Ent

Seducing Damian

Code of Honour
A Marriage of Convenience
The Lieutenant's Ex-Wife
A Man Like No Other
When Stars Collide

In Aeternum
Casanova in Training
Harbour of Refuge
Protected by Shadows
Polar Opposites

Theta Corps
Restitution
Contrition
Vindication

Interludes
Temporary Home
Alone With You
Till We Ain't Strangers Anymore

The Edge
Called Home to The Edge
Straying to The Edge
Returning to The Edge
Cuffed at The Edge

The Monroe Sisters
Need You Now
Let Me Go
I Won't Say Goodbye

Heart's Compass
The Princess and the Marquess

Flight of the Hawk
The Earl's Spark
His Unwanted Temptation

Keeper of the Stars
Part One
Part Two
Part Three
Part Four
Part Five

Astral Guardians
Chasing the Storm
Highlands at Dawn
Fields of Thunder
Branded by Frost
Driven by Night
Moon of Fire

Family Forever
Don't You Wanna Stay?
Love and Moonshine
First You Dream

Billionaire Brothers
Saving Rhodes
Lost Rhodes
Dangerous Rhodes

Shields and Sins
Preconception
Another Try

Collections
A Little Bit Cupid: This Ain't No Love Story
My Bloody Valentine: Perfect Duet

With Taige Crenshaw

Single Title
Unbreakable Bonds

Kemet Uncovered
Talios
Devi
Linc
Saffron
Taber
Ashia

Shields and Sins

ANOTHER TRY

ALIYAH BURKE

ENTWINED PUBLISHING

Another Try
ISBN # 978-1-80250-377-7
©Copyright Aliyah Burke 2026
Cover Art by Kelly Martin ©Copyright March 2026
Interior text design by Entwined Publishing
Published by Evidence, an Entwined Publishing imprint

This is a work of fiction. All characters, places and events are from the author's imagination and should not be confused with fact. Any resemblance to persons, living or dead, events or places is purely coincidental.

All rights reserved. No part of this book may be used, reproduced, or distributed in any form or by any means, including but not limited to electronic, mechanical, photocopying, recording, or by any information storage and retrieval system, without prior written permission from the publisher. This book and its contents are expressly reserved from use in training artificial intelligence technologies or systems. Furthermore, this work is expressly reserved from the text and data mining exception, in accordance with Directive (EU) 2019/790 of the European Parliament and of the Council.

Applications should be addressed in the first instance, in writing, to Entwined Publishing. Unauthorised or restricted acts in relation to this publication may result in civil proceedings and/or criminal prosecution.

The author and illustrator have asserted their respective rights under the Copyright Designs and Patents Acts 1988 (as amended) to be identified as the author of this book and illustrator of the artwork.

Published in 2026 by Entwined Publishing, United Kingdom.

Entwined Publishing is a division of Totally Entwined Group Limited.

ANOTHER TRY

Dedication

To the Ride or Dies! Everyone should be blessed enough to have one in their life.

Chapter One

The world breaks everyone, and afterward, some are strong at the broken places. ~ Ernest Hemingway

San Diego

The sun beat down on him without mercy and one-time decorated Detective Lance Baldwin of the Atlanta PD—now undercover lowlife, mob errand boy rising up the ranks as Lance Beckner—wiped the sweat off his brow and lifted the brown bottle to his lips and drank. The beer wasn't even cold any longer and he was so close to spitting it out and demanding another. Why? Because that's what his asshole persona would do.

Day in and day out he'd spiraled down further and further until it had gotten to the point of did he even recognize himself in the mornings when he stood in front of the mirror? His Italian silk suits may remain but he wasn't remotely close to the man he'd been a year and a half ago when he'd been tapped for this assignment.

And on the few rare moments he was honest with himself, he didn't think he ever would be again. All he knew was he needed to get out of here and back to his life.

A hand smacked him hard on the back and he didn't even grunt, aware that was what Michel Jankovic was going for.

The asshole lowered his bulk to the outdoor stool beside Lance and waved for a drink.

"Something happen for you to come seek me out on my time off?" He didn't get a lot of it and guarded it like a dragon and their treasure.

"Actually, Lance, your time is mine. If you have me on your ass for the next month, you'll accept it and do so with a goddamn smile."

Lance put down the bottle and shook his head and he slid from the stool onto his feet. "Wrong. I put up with you showing up on my ass like this purely because I work for your father. Even your old man figures I deserve some time. I mean, how am I supposed to get some pussy when I have your fucking ugly mug shadowing my ass? I don't do threesomes and you're definitely not my type."

Michel didn't appear all that dissuaded by his soliloquy. He belched and scratched his chest.

"Can't see at all why having you like a fucking anchor around my neck would hurt. Fuck, you can't even dress up to respect your father. I'm not looking for a five-dollar whore. I have more class than that and don't need to spend my days in line at the free clinic getting checked to make sure I'm disease free."

Lance pulled out a wad of money from his pocket, ripped off two bills, caught the bartender's gaze and dropped them down. The man nodded at him but didn't approach. In fact, he continued his conversation with another man.

"Leave me the fuck alone, Michel. I need to get laid with my woman and I'm not offering up classes on how to make sure your partner is satisfied or how to be more than a three-pumper."

Michel glared. "My women are satisfied."

Lance leaned close, anger tinging his tone. "You don't fuck women, you go after children. They can't speak for themselves." He inched nearer yet, daring the man to reach for him. "And if they could, they would tell you to stop."

He spun away, only to pause when a bearpaw clamped down on his arm. Michel was back in his face.

"You don't approve but you work for my father."

"Money is one thing but no, I don't see any reason to fuck a child when there are plenty of women who would even look past your lack of *everything* because you have money." He pushed his finger in Jankovic's chest. "Do *not* grab me again."

Lance walked off, aware he was making himself a target, inviting Michel to attack. When the attack didn't happen he was almost equal parts surprised and not at the result. Michel was a hothead and was well-known for losing his temper and beating people into little balls of pulp. Or having his bodyguards do it for him.

However he was also, and rightfully so, scared to fucking death of his old man. Lance had busted his ass to get to where he was. He hated it. And did so with every fiber of his being, but he had a job to do and he was going to continue doing it so he could bring this human trafficking empire down.

Burn it so not a single person in the family would ever think they could get away with it again in their life. Instill the fear of God, or the Devil, into them and make them shiver whenever his name was whispered.

A couple of blocks later he walked up to a different bar and ordered a drink. Nodding at the bartender, he made his way to one of the outdoor tables and took a seat beneath the brightly colored umbrella.

Women in bikinis sashayed by, some trying to pick up someone, others apparently just out in the perfect weather. A large shadow appeared in his periphery, but he didn't jump, didn't make any motion of surprise.

"My son says you are being disrespectful."

"Your son is a fucking idiot and will do nothing but get your business in trouble." Lance sipped his drink, still not looking over to the man who'd taken a seat at his table.

Again, there was no need.

"This is true." Dusan Jankovic gestured to someone, presumably to get a drink delivered. "However, he is my son and high up in my business." He glared at Lance with cold blue eyes. "Higher up than you."

Lance drained his drink and watched with zero interest as some barely clad honey dropped off a drink and exchanged a heavy kiss with Dusan. When they parted, his boss had one meaty hand down her bikini bottom, groping her ass and fingering her pussy with two digits.

"If you no longer want my work, say so. But don't insult me and say that I have to take orders from a man who thinks with his small dick. Your son is a detriment to the business that you're trying to grow. If that's who I have to follow, I will walk away right now because I'm not letting that man fit me for a pine box."

Dusan frowned, pulled his fingers from the girl's pussy, and smacked her on the ass. "Leave us."

She sauntered off on her too-tall six-inch heels.

"Explain these words to me, Lance."

"You want to discuss this here?"

Dusan shrugged. "They know who I am and what happens if they talk." He narrowed his eyes. "Like you do."

Just more reason to get this fuck off the street. This bastard was so arrogant the thought of discussing something like this in public didn't cause even the slightest bit of hesitation. Granted, it wasn't *anywhere* in public, but certain businesses.

In a way it made sense. The man had more spies than Lance wanted to think about. It sucked because being undercover here meant zero contact with anyone other than his handler, and those contacts were few and far between.

He was ready to finish this and move on. With what he wasn't sure, but this case had begun to take its toll on him, making him wonder if he needed to simply get out of the business altogether.

"Not sure how else you want me to explain it. Your son thinks he's untouchable. He's very vocal about the young girls who are picked up and sold. I've heard him going on about it to other girls, threatening their little sisters with phrases like, 'I can make them disappear' or any number of things that includes him actually fucking them." Dusan's gaze darkened but Lance pressed ahead. After all, the man had asked. "You have people loyal to you in the department, yes, but there isn't going to be anything they can do when your son mouths off in front of the wrong people. As powerful as you are, there are others in this city who hold more power. We both know this."

He sipped his drink, staring around the bar briefly, glossing over the women in their skimpy outfits both inside and outside of the establishment.

"Why have none of the ones around him come to me with this?"

Lance shrugged. "Can't speak for them in that regard. My guess would be that they have a job to keep him alive. They're loyal to him and answer to him."

"But you?"

"Like I said before..." He frowned as someone caught his attention. A tingle of recognition hit him, but she was gone seconds later, before the recognition could manifest into a name. "Like I said, I work for *you*. Not him. I told you when you came to me I wasn't taking orders from anyone else. Only you."

"What are you looking at?"

"Thought I saw someone I knew." He held Dusan's stare without blinking.

"Cop friend?"

Lance didn't worry, the man always wondered if people were cops. If they weren't on his payroll, he was suspicious. "Hardly. She was on this side of the law, drug running, carjacking, that kind of thing."

Dusan scratched his jaw. "She good?"

"One of the best." Lance shrugged. "Doesn't matter. She's not there and it may not have been her."

Even as the words fell, she stepped into view once more. *Damn it! It* was *her*. He'd recognize her anywhere. Ever since she'd propositioned him back in Atlanta to let her go instead of arresting her, he'd been unable to get her out of his head. Just another thing to be pissed about in the long line of things that angered him. Having a hard-on for the untrustworthy, partially psychopathic twin of a woman he'd been watching. Of course, at that time he had thought the woman under his watch was the crazy drugged-out one. But the second the real Jasmine had touched him, he'd knew it hadn't been her. Lance had felt like he'd been stabbed by a handful of lightning bolts at that simple contact. A feeling he'd been unable to forget.

"Does she have a name?"

"Yes, she does. *My woman,* who I haven't seen in a long time because you keep me busy."

"Didn't know you had a woman. And why would you say someone you knew instead of just that she was your girl?"

"I don't share my life with you. Like you point out all the time, there is work and there is family. Right now, I'm on the work side."

That woman he had identified, well, she was something all her own. A woman he would be smart to forget even existed.

And she was a piece of work for sure.

Jasmine Hoyer.

Someone was watching her again. She wasn't sure who it was. Yet. Jasmine pushed her hands into the pockets of her white jean shorts after she tucked some hair behind her ear. Moving slowly, she paused to look at some postcards. You could always find these items along a beach, even though it seemed they were dying in this modern age of doing it all on your phone. Seemed the art of sending a card was going the way of the dodo. Or her. Old and outliving her usefulness.

Personally, she loved them. The photos on them, the thought of just sending a little something to a person you cared about. She used to collect them.

A bemused snort fell from her lips and she shook her head. *I used to do lots of things I haven't done in years.*

Because it was too dangerous for anyone she remotely gave a damn about to be in contact with her, given her past and current situation, plus her husband wasn't exactly her number-one fan, she sent postcards. Never words on them but a photo. A large collection of them so she could send different photos from

Another Try

anywhere. And yes, while they could check the postmark, she wasn't overly concerned for her own safety. But for her twin and her family, she would deal with precautions.

She hardened her heart over the sister she'd just started knowing when she'd had to leave again. Jasmine had skipped witness protection because it hadn't been good enough for her the first time—she'd survived and she'd do so again. Plus, those government types were more apt to stab her in the back then actually help her. They'd done so before, why would she expect anything but the same the next time around?

"Can I help you with anything?"

She blinked and looked over to the small blonde in a teal bikini top and a deep peach floral sarong behind the counter. The color combination was stunning, in her opinion. And the blonde wore them well.

"Just trying to decide on the cards I want."

"Okay. We do have a few others on the rack by the other side of the tent."

Pulling two of her favorites, she put them on the counter as she moved to the other postcard stand and took another look. She didn't have the visual advantage from here, but she would still be able to see if she'd picked up a tail.

She didn't want to be here longer than necessary but a person could only spend so much time in a dingy room. If she was pinched, either by the locals who ran the area or the law, she had a card to play. Didn't want to, but could if needed.

With three more cards in hand, she went back to the counter and paid for the five cards and stamps as well as a pen. Waving off the need for a bag, she walked out into the sun once more and beelined it straight for a vacant table.

Staring over the cards, she picked her favorite and wrote down an address. One she duplicated on three of the other four. She walked away and put one in a blue mailbox as she moved by, dropping the pen in as well.

Angling herself in the direction of the larger crowd, she moved seamlessly with them, blending in and becoming one of the faceless enjoying the day on the beach and the boardwalk.

Jasmine fought a yawn and made a wide turn to head back to her place, having exhausted her daylight hours. She needed to hole up before the worst predators showed up. Finding a shortcut, she took it and bypassed a woman and her man who were about to do something for probably twenty dollars in the alley. Hopefully the woman had kneepads. Not that she would be there for long, he didn't look like a man who would last.

Hands shoved in her deep pockets, she had one curled around her ASP collapsible baton just in case. She had moved by a dumpster and neared the end of the alley when she was grabbed from behind and slammed against the wall, a hand over her mouth.

Her panic lasted all of five seconds, then the anger rose within her. In a single fluid, well-practiced move, she withdrew, snapped open her ASP and struck with it.

Her attacker cursed and released her. She took another swing at his upper body and connected with his forearm as he blocked the strike.

"Fuck you for picking on a woman," she exploded.

Jumping back, she turned her back and struck off.

"Jasmine!"

She'd not been called that in so long it took longer than it should have to process. Sad, considering it was nothing more than one word. Even on her stolen calls to her sister, her twin, she wasn't called that. There were no names, just all-too-short conversations.

All of her well-honed survival instincts screamed for her to jet. Bolt away from the hottie man she'd just whipped with her ASP, and yet that deep voice pulled at her, refusing to allow her feet to gain any momentum. Snapping the ASP out once more, she turned back and watched him warily as he pushed to his feet.

There was something very familiar about him but she couldn't place it. Her brain couldn't connect what she saw with anything from her memory banks.

"You have thirty seconds to tell me who the fuck you are and why you're trying to get my attention after attacking me."

His ball cap, while askew, hadn't been knocked free, so she was still unable to see his full features. There was a sexy layer of scruff lining his face and while it was nice to see, it only hindered her further from identifying this person. She wasn't a fan of not being able to see all his features but kept her cool. At least until two other men, large ones, turned the corner of the alley.

Fuck. Exactly what she'd been trying to avoid. She didn't want to be on anyone's radar. But she had made it her personal mission to know the names of the players around. Her safety depended on it.

"What happened, Lance? I see this bitch beat you. I think I may need a piece of that."

Michel Jankovic. Fucking scum but she knew who he was. Again, survival had dictated she know. She flexed her fingers around the ASP against her back leg, aware they couldn't see it. Taking on the son of Dusan Jankovic would be a death sentence but she wasn't going to go down without a fight.

Not like I haven't had that sentence over my head before.

Then there was the other man. The one she'd attacked. Michel had called him Lance.

Again a frustrating tingle of recognition teased her without mercy, but she still couldn't place him. She'd known a few Lances in her time. Some good, some most definitely bad. Others just running the middle.

Whoever he was, he moved closer to her, keeping up with the forward progression of Michel and his bodyguard. That one would be the one who had to get put down first.

"Just a bit of a disagreement between me and my woman. She's pissed I haven't been by in a while."

His woman? Did this fucker just lay claim to me? Why does that make parts of me that have been untouched for far too long sit up and take notice?

No accent to speak of in that delicious voice and damn it all, she was fucking intrigued. She didn't move away, instead moving closer to him. She didn't know who he was, but she was sure that he wouldn't attack her until he got what he needed from her.

Fairly certain.

Hopeful.

"She doesn't know her place then, if she doesn't think a man can go after all the whores he wants." Even though she couldn't see him, Michel's voice was unmistakeable.

The stranger shifted smoothly before her, blocking her view of either man. She narrowed her eyes at his back. Protection wasn't anything she had counted on from a man for a long time. "I didn't say she was a whore. I said she was *my woman*."

"Same thing."

He reached back and took hold of her arm. "Not to me. You're always so curious as to why I turn down the women you toss in my direction. This is why. I have a woman. I have pussy at home, so I don't need to go out and beg or pay for it."

Surely she had to be hearing things because it sounded to her like this man, one she didn't know, had just declared her *his* woman. *Guess my earlier thought was spot-on.* And he still held her like he meant it. She was pressed up against him and he'd wrapped his arm around her, settling it on her ass as if she'd not just beat him with her ASP and as if he had the right to touch her in such a manner.

Strange thing was, she was intrigued and didn't argue with him. While she didn't completely relax into him, she didn't fight him on the personal touching or his outrageous claim either.

"We don't like surprises," Michel barked.

"Again, I don't work for you. I work for your father. I'll introduce them when I'm ready."

Words that pushed alarm through her. Michel was bad enough, but if this guy was working for Dusan, she may be up shit's creek. Naked.

Michel crossed beefy arms. "Be ready now. I'm bringing in my father."

"Do what you must. I don't care, but step away and let me apologize to my woman without you trying to get some fucking lessons on how a man talks to a woman as opposed to what you usually do, interacting with a child."

Even more interesting by the second, things got.

The man watched the other two move away before he faced her again. Jasmine blinked, her fingers comfortable around her baton, just waiting for some wrong move. This time it wouldn't be a disabling blow but a deadly one. He shifted them a bit more but made sure he could keep an eye on the two men. She recognized the move.

"I need your help, Jasmine."

"I told you, I don't know you or who that person is you keep calling me. I think you had better tell your friends there you made a mistake."

His chuckle was deep and, fuck it all, arousing. He could have just pushed his hand down her pants and flicked her clit given how her body responded. Working her over completely and reminding her how long it had been since anything beyond her own fingers had been between her legs.

Not good.

"I know I didn't. Want to know how I know this? Because *you* propositioned *me*."

"I've done that to more than one man. It doesn't make you all unique or special."

That chiseled jaw flexed and a low rumble escaped. "You do that a lot to detectives?" He thumbed back the bill of his cap and she stared into his eyes. While they were no longer the icy green she remembered but blue-green, they were still intense as all get out.

Holy fucking shit and goddamnit. He may look a bit different, but no way would she *ever* forget this man. And, from the looks of things, he'd not forgotten her either.

Be that good or bad, it was something that remained to be seen.

One of Atlanta's own, Detective Lance Baldwin.

Chapter Two

Every moment of your life is a second chance.

It had been a risk. He knew that and understood it but he didn't care. Lance knew she could help him and he was willing to do what it took to secure that help. And he meant whatever. Thinking back over everything that Declan had said about her, he knew trusting her wasn't something he should just do blindly. After all, she'd set her own sister up.

Despite the fact that every nugget of information he'd read about her—and that had been a thick and a damn interesting read—and had had to deal with when their paths crossed, informed him this was a woman who spelled nothing but trouble for any male stupid enough to think with his cock around her. Or underestimate her.

She'd make them pay.

Even though she'd not been his informant or even his issue, he had been helping out Declan McBride and they had been on the steps of the courthouse on a nice sunny day when Declan's then-lover—and a woman whom everyone had thought was Jasmine—had reminded him she wasn't her. At all.

He'd been about to get back in his vehicle and back to his world of being a detective, not a babysitter, when the witness who'd everyone thought was Jasmine announced once more she wasn't and that Jasmine was over there. The similarities were there but Caro had a softness about her that Jasmine didn't. Jasmine's gaze was shrewd and never slowed as she constantly watched the world around them, even as her lips turned up in a mocking smirk.

Enter Jasmine. The real one. And the prosecuting ADA had been livid. She'd lit into both sisters after getting them into a small room, and while most people had watched Carolyn's responses, he'd been focused on Jasmine—the real Jasmine—and there hadn't been any way to disguise the rage that had flared in her gaze as she'd looked at the woman threatening her twin. It had taken him everything in him to ignore the heat that flared in his gut the longer he watched her. Caro did nothing for him but Jasmine, hell, he'd not wanted to focus on it. Given Declan had married Caro after he got his head out of his ass, he assumed it was the opposite for that man. Caro did it for him, not the real Jasmine.

So while on paper the woman had set up her own sister, he would be stupid to assume she didn't care about her.

"What do you want?"

Her tone had as much warmth as it ever had when they were back in Atlanta and she'd been dressed like a five-dollar hooker. Made him nearly reach for a winter coat as if they weren't in sunny California. Didn't matter then and it didn't now, there had always been something more to her. He would have bet his shield on it then, now he had something a bit more on the line. His life.

"I told you." Lance rolled his lower lip between his teeth.

She narrowed her eyes ever so slightly. "Lose your cushy gig in Hotlanta?"

He noticed that she continued to monitor where Michel and his asshole men had gathered. More arrived as they stood there, far enough away that their words weren't going to be overheard, but that Michel felt he still held some control.

Shifting his stance, he swallowed hard as his cock responded. "Something like that."

She popped the gum in her mouth and shook her head. "Fail to see how this is any concern of mine."

He moved his hand along her ass, fingers brushing just below the hem of the shorts she wore, exposing her sexy, toned legs. She trembled beneath his touch.

"What will it cost me?" The moment the words left his mouth, he realized there had been a million other, *better,* ways to ask her to keep his secret from the men gathered. But no, his mind, which didn't seem to work right when he thought about her, had gone on the fritz once again. *So of course I make sound like she is a whore and I want to hire her.*

The sneer on her face wasn't faked, and when she held up her hands, the men watching them laughed. His stomach twisted. This could very well be the end. The four men walked closer. He wanted to kick their asses and keep them away. He didn't have a solid on her cooperation and it made him nervous.

As fuck.

She shifted away from his touch and he disapproved of her move for more than one reason. Told himself the *only* reason that was important was he couldn't shield her if or when shit went sideways.

"You think that offering up some lame-ass apology is going to make up for this latest stunt you fucking pulled on me?" Her voice pitched higher, definitely carrying to those near, as she pulled her gum out of her mouth and smashed then stretched it between her thumb and index finger. She watched it as if it held all the secrets to the universe.

Lance latched onto that and prayed his instincts about her hadn't been wrong.

"Come on, baby. You know I have to go when my boss calls. I can't tell him no. I didn't *want* to be away from you for the past few nights. I *had* to be."

She scowled and flicked her gum in Michel's direction. The man scrambled back and glared at her. She shrugged her slender shoulders and turned toward Lance once more.

"I'm not sure you'll be able to pay what this will be costing you."

He saw a lifeboat and grabbed on the line it dragged without a second of hesitation. Shifting so they were again touching, he skimmed a hand down her face. The result was far from an act. Lightning crackled through him, his pulse skittered up, and not because of the men there. It all had to do with this woman. Blood zipped south and settled all too comfortably in his dick.

"Whatever it takes, baby. Just, please. No more ASP and forgive me. I'll spend all night on my knees for you if that's what it takes." A wicked grin. "You know how much I *love* being between your legs."

The men gathered laughed but he didn't take his gaze from her. There in her brown eyes was a spark of something he'd seen in her gaze the first day he'd met her. Coincidentally that had been the day she had propositioned him. In all his days of wearing a badge he'd never been so tempted to take someone up on an offer as he had been then.

She shifted to him, hips swaying with a seductive motion he knew people paid good money to learn. He would bet his life, and in a sense he was, that she came by hers naturally. Just like everything else about her. Natural.

He wanted to find out the truth.

His cock twitched when she walked her fingers up his chest to smooth them along his jaw. She stopped when her full chest brushed him and he would have had no problem shifting his hands a tiny bit and grabbing her hips or ass in his hands, hauling her flush to him.

Her touch along the facial hair he still hadn't had time to knock back was incredible. And he was even more fucking stupid than he had been. He didn't need to be losing his shit around her but getting her to help him and out of the situation.

All it took was her touch and he was rendered helpless.

"One night isn't going to be enough."

Isn't that the fucking truth.

"Whatever you want, baby." He brushed the back of his hand along her face. "Forgive me?"

"Maybe."

"My old man's here. Says he's ready to meet your bitch."

Jasmine growled, and in no more than five seconds had spun and kicked a can that launched through the air to hit Michel in the middle of his forehead.

"Don't fucking call me bitch." Her words were low and angry.

Lance tugged her back against him, this time not stopping as she'd done but making damn sure she was against *all* of him and experiencing all he offered. He also shifted to the left, keeping her out of Michel's direct line of sight.

"Fuck you, bitch. That hurt."

The red mark on his head had his men snorting even as they tried without success to keep it contained.

"I'm going to kill you." Michel's accent had thickened.

"No, you're not," Lance warned. "I told you she wasn't a whore but my girl. You're the one who insulted her. And in doing so, insulted me."

"You didn't say anything."

He tightened his grip on Jasmine's hip. "Trust me, I will protect my woman when she needs it. She is more than capable of handling herself."

"I said I was ready to meet. Why are you all still out here?"

Dusan brushed by the men and glared at them all. Then he paused and looked once more at his son.

"What the fuck happened to you?" he demanded. It was obvious he was unsure how to process what he was seeing.

"He called my woman a bitch one too many times." Lance flexed his grip along Jasmine's hip, needing her to remain still. Oh, and quiet. Definitely quiet.

While unsure on how the father would react to an assault on his son and knowing his ass was in deep shit if he lost progress on this case because he was protecting someone, he didn't care. Dusan looked at the woman against him, one hand pressed tight to his chest and the other by his back pants pocket. Lance had his arm around her, protective. Possessive.

"I like you, Lance. It is good for my boy to learn to mind his mouth and learn that not every woman he sees is one of his crack whores." The man strolled toward them, eyes roving over Jasmine.

"What is she into?"

"*She* is here and can speak for herself."

So much for her remaining silent.

He flexed his fingers in warning. Smarting off to the son was one thing. To Dusan? Not smart.

"Be quiet, woman." Dusan narrowed his gaze at her.

A derisive snort left her and she shook her head. "If this is the one that you kept leaving me for all those nights, then the two of you can fucking suck each other for all I care. I'm not going to be talked to by a man who has cops sniffing around his operation and is too fucking stupid to know." She shoved Lance's arm from her and got two steps before Dusan grabbed her.

"What the fuck are you talking about?"

Lance's bellow of protest was silenced as he watched all the color drain from Dusan's Slavic features. All his men were statues, hands poised on their weapons.

Jasmine didn't even flinch from the beefy hand gripping her arm in what had to be a bruising hold. "My own man grabbed me and I beat his ass with an ASP, what the fuck do you think I'm going to do when a human trafficker grabs me? Let me go or there will be a hole in you no one can fix. You'll bleed out before your men can muster their unsurprisingly few brain cells and get you to a hospital."

Well fuck, it may be more than the undercover op that is over. I could be about to lose my life. Lance waited for a moment to make his move.

Jasmine didn't blink or take her stare from the pale blue one holding hers. The anger that had burned in that gaze began to morph into respect and amusement. Then it came, the barest of lip twitches.

"You know of me."

Yes, you slimy piece-of-shit motherfucker. Of course I know you. I know all about you and what it takes to impress you.

She lifted an eyebrow and looked down her nose at him, even though he towered over her. "Of course I do. Anyone who wants to stay alive in this area knows you and your men."

He grinned and shifted only to freeze when she pushed forward with the nose of the Springfield Armory Hellcat Compact she held against his femoral artery.

Jasmine clucked her tongue. "I said I *know* of you. Nowhere in that statement does it mean I *trust* you."

"Lance. Tell your woman I won't hurt her." Dusan grinned and, honestly, she was a bit more concerned by *that* then his previous anger.

"Baby?"

Lance moved up beside her and hooked a finger in her belt loop before tugging. She appreciated how he didn't block her shot, and she was sure her detective was ready to draw down as well.

Wait. He's not mine.

Fuck.

Dusan continued to smile even after Lance had pulled her back, settling her against his chest, still giving her a shot if it became needed. She waited and Dusan looked back at his men. "It has been so long since someone has gotten the best of me." Back to her. "You need to come with me and tell me how you know of me. Perhaps I have work for you in my organization."

"Sorry, I don't deal in humans." More than a bit of derision in her tone. It told everyone there what she thought of him and those in his network for doing what they did.

Dusan sidled closer, eyes wide with curiosity.

"That statement implies there's something you do deal in." He stroked his hand along his clean-shaven jaw.

"Maybe I'm going clean." A small lift of her shoulders.

"Perhaps, but if that were the case you wouldn't be with Lance. That man is far from clean." He crossed his arms. "He doesn't mind getting his hands bloody."

The man at her back stiffened, not enough that those watching could see but she felt it. Even so, she didn't react. Instead, she shrugged and leaned deeper into his chest and patted Lance's cheek with her unarmed hand.

"He's my man and he's one who does what is needed. And right now, I'm in need of his cock. You've kept him from me for days. He has things to make up for and, believe me when I say, neither you nor your men are welcome to join in the fun."

"You will come tomorrow for breakfast and we will find a spot for you on my crew and you will tell me how you know there are cops watching me." He stroked his chin. "I want to make you come now."

"So do I," Lance grumbled, much to the amusement of all there. Even Michel eeked out a smile.

Pushing the gun in the waistband at her back, Jasmine tossed the head of the Jankovic crime family a rare smile. This was an arena she knew how to get muddy in. "I know things like that because I'm fucking good. Better, in fact. That's why I have no record and why cops can't catch me. I'm better than they are." The man at her back tightened his grip once. "I don't trust people and I *never* take people back to my place. We can talk if you want but I'm not riding with you, I'll follow along with my man."

Jasmine lifted her chin and glared at the group there. "Then afterward, I get him to myself for a full two days. I don't want any goddamn interruptions or him needing to go save your stupid sperm over there from some other shit he's gotten himself into."

"Most people are scared of me."

She was, but she'd also survived on her own after she'd been abandoned and had learned the hard way not to show fear. Jasmine blinked.

"I'm sure they are. Let's cut to the chase, you want to know about me. I, however, don't give a damn about you. Are we going now or do I get to go enjoy the cock that I've been missing because your son got grabby with his little fingers? And that resulted in him getting his pecker smacked by me so he tattled to you. Do you always fight his battles for him? I hope he's not the one you expect to take over this business of yours. He'll run it into the ground before you're even cold in your casket. Or hot in the lower realm of purgatory, not sure of how you are going to be taken care of."

He held her gaze and assessed her. "How is it you kept her from me, Lance? She is brash, yes, and totally without the respect I see in my women, but she is also not one who spends her days going to spas and spending money. She works like a man, behaves like one."

Lance grabbed her ass and planted a kiss on her neck. She shivered as he scraped his teeth along her pulse, knowing he felt it. Holy shit that was potent, and it hadn't even been on her mouth.

"Not all the time she doesn't."

All the men roared in laughter.

"I'm sure she knows how to ride your face and take your cock like a pro."

He vibrated behind her. "You'll never know because I'll *never* share her."

Relaxing into his ironclad hold, Jasmine sighed. "What's it going to be?" So much for her plans of laying low.

"We will talk tomorrow. Early. You know the time and place, Lance. Let's go home." He snapped his fingers and as one all the men turned except for Michel. At least not until his father smacked him in the back of the head.

After another glare, one she wasn't sure was for her or the sexy detective still curved around her like she was his everything, he stalked off after his father.

Alone in the alley once more, she angled back to him so they were face to face. She knew a siren's smile turned up her lips, she skimmed her hand down his chest until she gripped his cock, then she squeezed until she had his attention.

Holy fuck, the man had a size on him she would love to try out. His eyes roved over her face like he had permission to eye-fuck her.

"Wanna keep holding onto that, baby? Or are we going to get out of this alley and start making up for lost time?"

She dragged her tongue along her lower lip and loved how his eyes darkened with heat. "I've not held it for so long. You know I go through withdrawals." She began stroking him. His large frame shuddered seconds before he curved his hand around the back of her neck. Strong fingers bit into her flesh, marking her. Claiming her.

Problem was, she didn't mind.

"I have no problem fucking you here." His words were rasped.

"Is that fucking me? Or fucking me over?"

He lowered his face and brushed his mouth along the corner of hers. "We need to talk, but they're still watching us."

Yeah, she wasn't an idiot.

Nipping at his lip, she sucked it into her mouth and ate his groan as he grabbed her hips, smashing their bodies together. Need sizzled through her, so powerful she almost forgot she stood in a darkened alley with a man she'd once propositioned mostly so he wouldn't arrest her.

Another bite to his lip and she pulled back to see his eyes. "Your place, because I'm not taking you to mine." She released his cock and put a couple of steps between them.

Chapter Three

Trusting you is my decision,
but proving me right is your choice.

Back at his place, Lance ran a check for listening devices, even though the steps he'd left in place to make sure no one had entered while he'd been out meeting Michel then Dusan were still in place. He couldn't afford not to be extra vigilant. While he did, Jasmine leaned against the wall. Not the door, but the wall that was behind cement, not trusting just a small bit of wood to keep her safe if a shot came. He admired her for that.

He was bothered by a few things. First was that she didn't speak and didn't seem to be in any rush to do so. The second and far more important aspect was the intensity of his attraction to her.

Content with his check, he exhaled and rested his head against the wall. "Can I get you anything? Drink? I have water, beer, and juice."

His place wasn't that big, and he didn't spend a lot of what was given to him. Part of his way to not get comfortable with the life.

"No."

He stared at her before pushing away from the wall and heading to the kitchen for a drink. She may not want or need one, but he sure the fuck did. Popping the top on his beer, he strolled back into the living room. Jasmine hadn't moved.

"I need your help."

Again, not a peep from her. The first time, and last, that they had been together, her mouth hadn't stopped moving as she'd cussed out the ADA, another cop, and probably him. He couldn't remember everyone who'd gotten a taste of her wrath.

This woman here, now, was different than that one. No horribly clashed outfits. No hair that looked like it belonged back in the eighties. While she wasn't as subdued in clothing choices as her twin, it was so much less than it had been.

Those large brown eyes of hers watched him.

"Are you going to say anything?"

"Who are you undercover with?"

He flattened his lips, knowing he wasn't supposed to say a fucking thing.

A shake of her head. "Want my help but you don't want to tell me anything. Fine. How about I tell you what I know." She pushed from the wall and moved toward him, hips doing that damn evocative sway that he no longer doubted was natural. Her movements were too sensual no matter the situation to be anything but.

"You're under with the Feds because they think they'll be able to bring that fuck down. Problem is, you're starting to lose it because you've been under so long. Doubting what you hear, not sure who you can trust any longer, and you want out. So much so you're actually risking it all to reach out to someone outside your little circle. And you're hoping that I'll go along with this stupid plan of yours."

She was right there in front of him and he pulled her the rest of the way in so he could take possession of her pillowy lips.

Jasmine didn't play coy with him, not in the slightest. Her mouth opened to welcome in his questing tongue. He licked all he could, the sides and top of her mouth, before dancing his tongue with hers. Her taste was something he would never forget — jasmine and a hint of oranges.

He growled low and cupped her ass, lifting her into his arms. She immediately wound her legs around him and he backed her into the wall. Jasmine threaded her fingers into his hair as she rotated her hips, rubbing her pussy along his cock. His senses were flying out of control. Lance swore her heat singed him through his jeans and her shorts.

Reaching between them, he put his hand over her core. Her response was to buck her hips farther into his touch farther. He nipped at her lower lip and pulled back to see her eyes, dark and hazy with desire. He realized this was a look he enjoyed on her. A lot.

He rubbed his knuckle along the seam of her shorts, pushing a bit harder when he was over her clit. Her full lips parted and she whimpered, not once dropping her gaze from his.

"What do you want?" His question was barely more than a rumble.

"Touch me." Jasmine panted.

He gave her another two strokes while he did his level best to ignore the cock threating to punch free of his denim.

"I am." He nipped her chin. "Tell me what you want."

"Your fingers in my pussy. Make me come." She gasped as he rubbed harder. "Yes, God, like that. But more."

"You're going to come. More than once." He teased her smooth skin under the shorts as he angled closer to her heated center.

"Yes."

His dick pulsed as he came in contact with her smooth pussy, her arousal making her slick.

"Bare."

"Better this way." A shudder. "More sensitive."

Jealousy bit him at the thought of another touching her and having permission to enjoy what she offered him now. He shoved it away and dragged his fingers up her wetness. Her lids fluttered closed as another panted 'yes' fell from her mouth.

"Watch me, Jasmine."

Her fingers gripped his hair harder, nails digging into his skull as she listened to him.

"You're to keep your eyes on me. I want you to know who's doing this to you." He pushed two fingers deep in her heat and she moaned even as she bit her lower lip.

"Christ you're so fucking tight. You're going to choke the fuck out of my cock when I'm inside you."

Her nipples poked against the thin barrier of her shirt. He didn't fucking know where her ASP was and, right now, didn't care. Pumping his fingers, he worked her clit with the pad of his thumb.

Using the wall behind her to his advantage, he slipped his hand that wasn't being hugged by the hottest sheath he'd experienced to her breast and tweaked her nipple.

She came hard with a keening cry, legs lashing tighter around him. *Holy shit.* His legs shook with need and he fumbled with the fly on his jeans.

Shit. Condom.

Jasmine sucked her lower lip in her mouth and brought herself closer to his face. Brown eyes full of so much emotion and heat bore into his as she scraped along the nape of her neck with those short, unpolished nails of hers.

"Hurry."

One word. Barely over a whisper. He more felt the brush of her breath along his wet lips than heard the plea. It wasn't smooth, there wasn't any finesse as he ripped open the condom, rolled it down his hard throbbing length and drove deep into her seconds after he tugged her clothes to the side.

"Shit yes!" She bowed her back with the cry that escaped.

"Fuck me." He put them forehead to forehead as he held still, balls-deep inside her. "Christ, Jasmine. You're so fucking slick and tight. So goddamn tight."

She flexed her internal muscles and that just about kicked him over the edge of the control he struggled to maintain.

"Don't let me down now, Lance. I'm not looking for gentle lovemaking."

That was what he'd needed to hear. There wasn't going to be anything gentle about this. Far too long since he'd lost himself in a woman, and for it to be this one, who had always retained a hold on his memory? Raw. Hard. Fast. Deep.

Those were the words ripping through his head as his control eroded.

At the first hard thrust, she nipped his neck and begged for more. He gave it to her.

* * * *

It was the click of his doorknob that alerted Lance to potential trouble. Jasmine lay in his arms and they were on the floor in his bedroom. He flexed his fingers along her arm and smiled when she put his sidearm in his hand, all without moving much.

His perfect woman. They hadn't been so far gone to forget the need to have protection close.

The bedroom door flung open and Michel pulled up short. Lance got it, the man who believed himself invincible and untouchable had to be shocked to see himself facing down not one but two guns.

"What the fuck are you doing in my place, Michel?"

"Dad wanted me to bring you in." His beady eyes drifted back to the woman in Lance's arms.

"Keep your eyes off my woman." Lance spat out the words.

Michel adjusted himself. "You should share her. Is she not worth the bed? I see a lot of clothing all over your floor."

Lance sat up, allowing the blanket to fall to his waist. Looking to his left, where Jasmine had the cover tucked under her full breasts but the gun out and pointed with unerring accuracy at Michel, Lance smiled. Bending, he kissed her then stood up, naked.

A low moan from Jasmine hit him and he smirked. Then turned his back on Michel, trusting her to keep him safe. And the move showed off the rake marks she'd put on him as he went to draw on a pair of workout pants.

"Did you want to tell your dad why you had to stay and watch me dress? Or can you step out of the room so my woman can get dressed? I don't give a fuck if you look at my cock but I'll fucking be dead before I allow your eyes to rest upon her nude body. That's *mine.*" Lance didn't even attempt to hide the blatant possessiveness in his tone.

* * * *

Jasmine sank against the buttery-soft leather seat in the back of the SUV they rode in. Personally, she wasn't a fan of not having her own way out other than running, but it was too late for her to insist on getting there herself. Hell, she'd not had a car in years. Easier to be tracked down, and so much easier to just boost what she needed when and if she required it.

Lance sat beside her, his face the epitome of calm, but she knew better. She could read him like a book. Had been able to since the first day they had met. Jasmine hid a chuckle as she recalled his expression when she'd dragged her far-too-long nails up his chest and propositioned him.

Despite the line she'd crossed when she'd been betrayed, there were some things that had been imbedded deep in her soul. And leaving this man to face a certain death if she ratted him out wasn't something she could do. So for the moment she was officially the unofficial girlfriend of Lance, who worked for the Jankovic crime family.

She couldn't stop playing in her head how he'd protected her body from Michel's view. Like she actually meant something to him.

If only that were true, but I know my lot in life and it's not the happily ever after. Even if I do want it.

He reached across the space between them and picked up her hand, lacing their fingers.

"You okay, baby?"

Aware of the eagle-eyed stare of Michel, who continually turned around to watch them as if he couldn't help himself, she smiled and squeezed his hand.

"Of course. I'm with you. I mean, breakfast would have been nice, but I'm guessing you're going to *feed* me after."

Those kissable lips turned up and she realized, in that moment, that this could be a bad thing. There could be actual feelings forming for this man.

"I plan on *feeding* you many more times today, baby. My word on that."

She dragged her fingernail along his skin and watched his eyes darken.

Yeah, this had the potential to fucking blow up in her face.

Michel gave a snort of disdain before turning up the music. She grinned at Lance but didn't try to move closer to him and whisper. No doubt that's what Michel wanted them to do.

The ride took about thirty minutes with the traffic and she shifted on the seat when the luxury SUV slowed to turn into the Jankovic home. Home? Mansion was more apt a description. At least fifteen thousand square feet, and that was an assumption from seeing what she could from the long driveway that widened out to a circle at the front entry that had a damn stone fountain there. The large, vibrant green lawn beside them on either side was perfectly manicured with flowers, shrubs and hedges.

She waited after they parked for Lance to reach toward her, offering his hand. Taking it, she slid over the leather and climbed out to stand beside him, resting her palm against his chest as he settled his arm around her, his lips to her head.

"We'll be fine."

Not bothering to answer him, she walked beside him, quiet, as they approached the front entrance. The driver opened the door and she let go of Lance's hand so he could enter before her. Michel stepped up beside her and she bit back her growl of impatience and disgust.

"First time a woman of your color has walked through the front door. Usually they come in through the back to work."

Turning toward him, she pushed him into the wall by the entrance, finger on the gun that pressed into his dick.

"Yet you still hunger for the pussy you'll never get. Tell me, out of all those innocent girls you rape, how many look like me? We both know you want it but we're smarter and refuse to go with you, so you're relegated to rape, pedophilia, and porn to get your fix. I know this is your dad's house, but you fucking disrespect me again and I won't care what happens to me when I kill you." She pushed harder on the gun in his crotch. "Do we understand each other? I'm not your bitch and I won't be spoken to like shit on your shoe. Believe that."

"Baby?" Lance's deep voice flowed over her. "Should I be concerned that you're so close to Michel?"

"Of course not. You know I like men with meat between their legs. From what I can tell, he's struggling for two inches." She didn't look away from Michel as she spoke, instead holding his gaze and seeing the single bead of sweat that trickled down his face between his eye and nose.

"Let's go."

"Be right there." Another jab. "Do we understand each other? I know words are hard so just blink twice if you understand exactly what I'm saying."

Two slow but deliberate blinks came.

She knew her smile hovered far closer to a feral snarl crossed as she stepped back, hiding her gun as she turned her back on Michel and returned to Lance, who watched with a mixture of anger and... Was that jealousy in his gaze?

He snaked an arm around her, kissed her once and led her inside the opulent home.

"Damn." The word slipped from her lips.

"Yeah, thought the same thing the first time I was here." Another kiss to her temple. "Let's go, and please stop antagonizing his son."

She didn't respond to that, just let him lead her over white marble floors. The décor in here was enough to make her wonder if this house ever had a child running through these halls, it looked coldly perfect and she doubted they did. If the art and paintings hanging weren't originals, they were damn good replicas. The custom lighting and window treatments added to the opulence.

Dusan sat behind a large, dark-mahogany desk as they walked in his office, his expression serious as he looked them both over. The furniture filling the rest of the space matched — dark, heavy, upholstered wood.

"You look like you just got up."

"Your son interrupted our morning. Trust me, being here in front of you wasn't on our list." Lance rubbed his hand up and down Jasmine's back.

"You can leave, Lance. I wish to speak to your woman."

"Fine." He tipped her face up to his, eyes direct and honest. "I'll be out there waiting, baby. You need me, you call."

She smiled and rested her hand on his torso. Not because she *wanted* to touch him, of course. All for the ruse. Right?

Right.

Right.

Shrugging as if she didn't have a care in the world, she pushed up on her toes for a quick kiss. "I'm sure we'll be fine. Although not sure why he wouldn't want you to hear who I have pegged as a cop. But...not my business."

She went to a chair and sat down, slouching back, legs spread, one arm along the back as if she didn't have a care in the world. Truth was, she was fucking freaked out. But hell, this wasn't anything new for her.

The man before her watched her with the same intensity she gazed upon him. Many people had their assumptions about this man. In truth, they had them about heads of crime families and those who were involved in the shit this one was. Thing about it though, this man was fucking smart.

There had to be a reason, more than luck, that he'd not been caught or stopped. And she knew it and wasn't foolish enough to think that she could talk to him like she had the previous night. She bet that he had a weapon on her or Lance right now to have the upper hand should her mouth get out of control.

He watched her, his blue eyes cold and shrewd. Dusan Jankovic wasn't an overly large man, his body was not small but wiry with lean muscles. She didn't flinch as he leveled what she realized he considered his "I'm going to make you squirm" stare.

Hah.

Joke was on him because she'd faced down far scarier than this man. And she excelled at the waiting game.

Five minutes of silence stretched between them, after which he lifted one black eyebrow.

"You aren't scared of me." He tipped his head to the side. "Why aren't you scared of me? I've never met a woman who wasn't. Even my wife is scared of me."

She blinked slowly, weighing her words. "I've been through enough shit in my life to only be scared of a few things. I'm also not foolish. I know you're a dangerous man, Mr. Jankovic."

His lips twitched and she knew that was what he had been wanting. He twirled a finger in her direction and she took it as a sign to continue.

"We both know you put up with my behavior last night because of Lance. I appreciate that. I don't like people getting in my personal space but I should have been," she paused, making a moue with her mouth, "a bit more careful."

"Not going to say anything about my son?"

She flashed a grin that wasn't the slightest bit nice. "The words I could say about him wouldn't be the slightest bit flattering."

"He is a bit of a twat." A shrug. "He's my son."

Those words that weren't uttered were—I have to love him.

Dusan leaned forward. "What about your parents? Do they know that you're on this side of the law?"

As always when undercover, it was best to stick close to the truth. "My parents got rid of me when I was a baby. Grew up in the foster system."

He nodded but didn't speak.

"A lot of time in and out of juvie before I ran away from the final home." Chills skittered down her spine and she willed them away, not wanting this man to see her weakness. Yet at the same time, she wanted to get it off her chest, and chances were that this man would not judge her any more than he already was doing.

"The husband in the home and the eldest boy decided that I was there to be their plaything."

"How did you meet Lance?"

If he expected to throw her by the change of subject, again, he underestimated her. Like most men did.

"It was a few years ago. Six or seven, I believe." She flicked a smile. "I propositioned him. Man wasn't amused at all."

Dusan laughed. He continued to do so as he rose from his desk and walked to the door.

"Come in here."

Lance stepped into the doorway and, damn it, her breath caught. How did this man make her feel such a way? By all rights she should toss his ass under the bus and get out of Dodge.

Last night sat vivid in her mind. His touches. Caresses. How fucking full he made her when he pushed home.

Lance's blue-green eyes lasered directly to her. She gave him a small nod, letting him know she was okay. He walked behind Dusan and paused at her chair, dipping his head to brush a kiss along her mouth.

"Hey, baby."

She didn't speak, just smiled.

Dusan settled back behind his desk. His eyes still twinkled and she hated that she was figuring he wasn't all that bad of a guy. He had charm. And given what he did to keep his family and his empire, she should despise the entire family with the heat of a hundred thousand suns.

And she did, but yet, she didn't know if she'd met him with him being unknown that she wouldn't have liked him. More reason to be disturbed.

"Your woman was telling me she propositioned you when you first met. When was that again?"

Lance shook his head. "She did. I was pissed. Thought she was a hooker." He picked up her hand and stroked his thumb along the back of her hand. "It was seven years ago. Didn't see her again for a few years, and that meeting was pretty much just the same as the first."

"I did *not* proposition you that time."

His lips twitched. "No, you surely didn't. I wanted to proposition you."

Dusan looked between them and she knew what he hunted for. Any stress or strain on their faces. She figured the man was pretty damn close to a human lie detector, which meant Lance was fucking awesome for still being there. And alive.

"The cops in my employ?"

Danger threaded along his question. Apparently the pretend we give a damn portion of the visit was over.

Chapter Four

If you're going through hell, keep going.
~ Winston Churchill

Lance hated the entire fucking thing. Sure, they were both armed, but there wasn't any way they would be able to overpower all Dusan's men if it came to a shootout.

He cut his gaze to the woman beside him. After this—he was being fucking optimistic that they would get out—he had to meet with his handler and tell them she was also imperative to it all. While he didn't expect that to go over well, he knew his handler and the agency wouldn't want to ruin his two years under.

"Why don't you tell me who you have on your payroll so I don't accuse them."

"You think I am going to tell you that?"

"And you think I'm just going to blurt out what I know without any sense of security? What do I get for this?"

"How about you get to stay alive?"

Jasmine's eyes narrowed as she leaned forward. "Go ahead and kill me then. You'll know you still have cops that are undercover without your knowledge and it will eat you alive. Especially when you're brought down. You'll just be like, if only I had listened to Jasmine and not tried to strongarm her."

Beside her, Lance gripped the arm of his chair but didn't move. Still, Dusan noticed and he pinned his sharp gaze on him—the man who'd infiltrated his crew.

"Nervous, Lance?"

"Of course I am," he retorted, barely stopping the eye roll. "My girl is challenging you to kill her."

"Make her stop." Dusan's eyebrow rose with that statement.

Jasmine and Lance both snorted at the same time and Lance shook his head. "You've met her. She took an ASP to me because she was pissed. I can't tell her to do anything."

The smile was fleeting but there. "True." A deep breath. "How about this. You tell me and I let you two have your weekend without any bother from the family?"

Lance captured her hand and skimmed his thumb along the back of hers. "Come on, baby."

"Fine." She shrugged. "Give me a piece of paper and I'll write it down."

Dusan pushed a pen and pad toward her. "Not worried about me running your prints?"

"Nope." She popped the p. "I already told you. I'm not in the system." She picked up the pen and clicked it before putting the tip to paper. For a brief second, she lifted her head and looked Dusan directly in the eyes. "They will swear they aren't cops, of course you know this. So before you ask me to prove the names, I'm putting down a time and date that you need to go to the bar they are in and watch who they talk to. The men listed here on different occasions, but same location, are both cops. Neither will be in uniform. You'll see a napkin slide between them each time. Don't go after the handlers, but do what you will with the traitors." Jasmine focused back on the sheet and for a few charged moments the scratch of the pen on paper was the only sound.

She pushed the paper back to him. "I don't want more cops to come swarming if you take out those two. But they are undercovers, they can't come after them."

Dusan lifted the sheet and swore. His gaze snapped back to Lance. "Your woman is impressive. And evil. I'm almost liking her more than you. Even before she's been vetted all the way by my people. I'm taking her photo to my man in the police and you'd better hope it all comes back as you said." The warning in Dusan's words was crystal.

Lance stood and brought her with him. "I know. We'll let you handle your business. Thank you for keeping your word."

"I'm many things but a liar isn't one of them. Have Sathal drive you back."

"Yes, sir."

Lance led her to the door, his large hand settling upon the small of her back. He wanted it there when she had no clothing on.

"Jasmine."

She slowed at the sound of her name and glanced over her shoulder. "Yes?"

"I'll be seeing you again. You and I could have a beautiful partnership."

She cocked an eyebrow. "I'm more of a one-woman man." A smile. "Now. Have a good day, Mr. Dusan."

Sliding her hand into Lance's back pocket, she kissed his cheek. "Let's go. You owe me some dick."

"I'm nothing if not a man of my word." Dipping his head, he nipped her earlobe before flicking his tongue along it.

Her sharp gasp soothed him for the moment. The ride back to his place was done with their hands roaming all over each other, kicking their arousal higher. They stumbled out of the SUV and into his place, where they stopped and held each other's gaze.

He gestured around the room and she nodded.

"Come on, baby. I need you," she panted as she walked away from him, checking that side of the room for any listening devices. Lance wasn't sure where she'd had the bug detector on her person but she had one in her hand.

"Then fucking get naked." He kicked off his shoes, making sure to direct them into the wall for added sound. "Or did you just want me to take you up right where you are?"

She angled her head to look at him and cocked an eyebrow. He winked even as he shrugged without repentance.

"Wall. Definitely the wall." She released a cock-hardening moan.

He watched her as she looked in the lamp on the small table. This time when she met his gaze, he knew she'd located one. Lance doubted that was the only one they'd left. Typically they left three.

Her hand slapping the wall snapped his focus right back to her. This was not going to be easy.

If they were giving out Oscars for this, she would earn hers. Right now the groans sliding from her weren't cutting him any slack. His dick ached so fucking intensely he didn't know how much more he could take without undoing his pants just to get some relief. The air filled with her moans, each one more passionate than the last. And the kicker? They fucking sounded so real they were about to get him off.

His eyes drifted closed only to snap open a bit later when she cupped his hardness through his jeans. He glanced down at her.

"I found two," she mouthed.

He couldn't think, just blinked.

Her hand slipped inside his jeans and the low growl of want, this time from him as she curved her hand around him.

"Why pretend?" Jasmine whispered.

The growl that fell would have been her only warning, had he not already been on her. Mouths fused together, he backed her right into another wall, the sound loud. Clothing flew off and she knocked over that same fucking lamp she'd found a device in as she scrambled to brace herself when he shoved deep inside her pussy with a single stroke.

He didn't care, she could break every single thing in there so long as *this* didn't stop. And from the way her fingers dug into his back, he could say with fair certainty it wasn't going to stop anytime soon.

* * * *

Hours later he paused outside the old warehouse where he met his handler, Jasmine beside him in jean shorts and an oversized surfing shirt to hide her weapons. He wasn't sure how this was going to go but his gut wasn't completely on board.

Not that he feared betrayal from her. He couldn't explain why he trusted her, however he did. But he knew how things went in the agency.

"I think, once more for the record, this is a mistake." Jasmine's words were matter of fact.

He clenched his jaw, wishing for there to be a bit more light, which would have allowed him to see her face better. "I refuse for this to go down and them think you're on his side. It's not going to be a quiet, tidy wrap-up. When this happens, it's going to be fast, loud and bloody."

"So I won't be there when it does. But you will." She shook her head. "I don't like this."

He cupped her face. "Trust me?"

Her bark of laugh, while hushed, didn't give him any relief. Didn't she trust him?

"Jasmine?"

She shook her head. "*If* I were to trust anyone with a badge other than my brother-in-law, it would be you."

Which meant she didn't trust him. That hurt. A lot.

The pain the knowledge brought him was an emotion he didn't have the time to try to figure out why or where it came from.

They walked in from the back and he led the way to a small room in the center where lights could be on but not seen from the outside of the building. He knocked twice, waited five seconds, then pushed the door in. After it clicked behind him a low lamp came on, allowing him to see his handler.

"You."

His handler spit that in his direction. No, correction. In Jasmine's.

They knew each other?

Fuck. They knew each other, and it didn't look as if there was going to be a lovely reunion.

Jasmine swung to the right instinctively as Lance moved left. No way it could be anything but instinct, for her eyes and one hundred percent of her focus had landed on a man she hadn't believed she would ever see again.

Robert Gibson.

Insides a righteous mess, she maintained her cool and aloof façade. His appearance hadn't changed all that much. A bit grayer, a bit heavier, but he still had enough of a presence for her to know he wasn't a man to ignore.

"What the fuck are you doing here?" His words were snarled. "Lance? Why are you with her?"

The urge to strike out rode her. Hard. But Jasmine had learned years ago about not tipping one's hand. One fist in her pocket, she allowed herself to brace against the wall with an arm and her fingers to skim the matte butt of her sidearm.

"She saved my ass with Dusan. Where do you two know each other from?"

She still wasn't opening her mouth. Waiting. Watching. Gathering intel, that's what she did now. And she was damn good at it.

Robert shook his head. "We can't risk this operation on her, she's a loose cannon. I'll take her in—we can release her when you're finished."

You have another think coming if you believe I will willingly let you take me into custody.

"Not happening. We had a meeting with Dusan this morning. The two of us. She vanishes and there will be more questions. He likes her more than he does me."

Disgust filled Robert's features. "His kind always like whores."

Lance shot her a brief look but she ignored the piercing stare, not risking taking her gaze from Robert.

"She's not a whore. How do you know each other?"

Lance moved between the two of them. She didn't want to notice — did, just didn't want to — that he stood closer to her than Robert.

"What'd she tell you?"

"Nothing. I just told her she had to come meet my handler. I don't want her getting hurt if she's there when this goes down."

"She won't be. Running is what she does best."

Red. Blood red, dripping down her face, none of it hers. Tears pooling as she wiped off the blood from her best friend, filled her vision. Her control began to erode and she bit the inside of her cheek to yank herself from the painful memory.

"I don't need this. Good luck with Dusan." Her words dripped ice.

Jasmine headed to the door. Lance snagged the beltloop of her jean shorts and held her there.

"She's staying. This woman is now part of my cover. This is happening, so deal with it. Both of you." Lance's words were decisive and firm.

He moved his hold from shorts to wrist.

"Stay." A command.

Eyes locked on Robert, she waited. More was sure to come, she knew it.

She held Lance's gaze then gave him a small nod before retreating to her spot along the wall. *Wonder if he'd have a heart attack if he knew that I'd fucked his man. More than once.*

"You can't fucking be serious right now. You've been in for almost two-plus years. Suddenly this girl comes in and you think she's your way in? Stop thinking with your dick. You want to fuck the slut, go ahead. But she will *not* be part of this."

"She already is and don't fucking call her a slut. Dusan bought her as my girlfriend."

"How?"

She waited for the retelling of her going after him with an ASP.

Caro would like that story. Maybe. Probably be a bit worried then she would laugh. She missed her sister, even though they weren't the closest twins.

"It is what it is," Lance growled. "If it came down to it right now, I'm sure he would take her over me. She gave him some information he wanted."

A derisive snort. "Of course she did." Robert's glare hit her. "Sell your soul?"

"I leave all that to you and your mentor, Satan." She stared at her nails before pushing that hand back in her pocket.

"You fucking gave up cops to that asshole?" Robert thundered as he stomped toward her.

Lance edged between them, his hard body protection she didn't want or need.

"Stop this." His order came to her low and graveled. "We can't waste time fucking around your past issues."

"I didn't give up cops. I gave him two of his son's men who are ratting to cops. Unlike you, Robert, I don't betray those whose back I'm supposed to have. Again, something that is far more up your alley than mine."

Anger flowed in her veins. All the years of trying to let it go faded away and it was as if her history had happened to her yesterday. Dropping her hand to the

ASP at her side, she lunged toward Robert only to be brought up short. Lance had a hold of her around the waist and he drew her against him. At least she got the pleasure of seeing Robert flinch back in fear.

She lowered her hand with the weapon in it. Lance plucked the ASP from her grasp and slipped it back into her pocket.

"Let's not do this. We have to be going, Robert. I'll send information when I can, letting you know the when and where."

She wouldn't trust the fucker as far as she could throw him. Biting her tongue to keep her personal opinion contained, she stepped away from Lance's touch. Only once she had retreated to the wall did her breathing come a bit easier.

Jasmine knew herself to be better than this. *If you hate a person, then you're defeated by them.* Repeating one of the many Confucius quotes she'd memorized, she eventually was back in a place of workable rage.

Keeping her comments to herself as they finished talking, she left without hesitation when Lance sent her the silent communication. She maintained her distance while he and his handler had their lover's quarrel, but she returned to his side when he beckoned.

Jasmine didn't allow her mask to slip, not for a single instant. When the trio parted and the two of them were walking on the way back to Lance's place, he dropped his arm around her shoulder and brushed a kiss over her cheek. Damn her body for standing up and waving for more. It was nothing more than a game, and if he didn't need her help, this wouldn't be happening.

My life isn't destined for what Caro has. It's to be alone and looking over my shoulder for the rest of my life.

Still, she knew how the game was played, and when they stopped at a street vendor for hot dogs, she didn't argue who paid, or the second kiss he took. They ate quickly and disposed of the trash before he held out his hand for her. Ignoring her voice of self-preservation that yelled this was going to hurt in the end, she took it.

Back at his place, they did another sweep before he turned on the radio, some oldies station, and tugged her into the small kitchen.

"Want to tell me what that was all about?"

"Nope."

"Tough shit." He gripped her chin and brought her face around to meet his. "I need to know."

Cutting off her arm may be less painful than revisiting these old memories. He was right, she owed it to him. Okay, that wasn't true, she didn't owe this man anything, she was doing this to help him, not because he was helping her.

Orgasms not withstanding.

"I'm going to need a drink."

He got her a beer and popped the top on it prior to handing it over. Her body trembled from the ever-so brief contact with his. Eyes locked to Lance's, she took a long slow drink, buying herself a bit more seconds before it came time to rip off that scab.

"I used to wear a badge. Had my training at the Farm but was immediately tapped for undercover work."

Yeah, this was going to fucking suck.

Chapter Five

Without memory, there is not healing.
Without forgiveness, there is no future.
~ Desmond Tutu

The Farm. Two words he'd never expected to hear out of Jasmine's mouth. Hell, when they'd first met and she'd looked like a junkie, that's what he'd assumed and he'd rolled with it. Even at their last meeting at the courthouse, he still wouldn't have pegged her to be someone who'd had the training he'd gotten later.

He didn't push her, gave her the extra time it was obvious she needed. And not just her. Lance swigged some back as well, needing a few additional moments to wrap his head around this.

Even when the silence dragged on, he waited, the pain in her eyes too real for him to ignore.

"I was good." Her voice low but shaky. "Damn good."

He could see the truth in her simple words. This woman held herself to a standard he never would have expected when he first met her. Still, he hated the pain that lingered even though he had no doubt she worked hard to erase it. And that knowledge she was still hurting after all this time, whatever the reason made him want to fix it for her. There existed something deep inside Lance that made him want to pull her into his chest and hold her. Give her his strength. Protect her. *Possess* her. Locking down his limbs, he didn't move. While the comfort would be offered, this woman was a firecracker in his arms and it would change to something sexual and he needed to hear this from her. Had to know what was going on.

Even so, he didn't rush her. This revelation wasn't something he would ever force her to divulge at the speed he wanted. He had to let her pick her own.

"We had an op in," a shrug, "guess it doesn't matter where it was. Multi-agency, blah blah, you know how it goes. Typically, the more letters involved, the stickier the situation becomes." A deep breath. "And the more likely it is for a leak."

He *really* didn't like where this was going.

"There *was* a leak, and the entire op went sideways. Not just a little oops, we have a bit more paperwork to do and make it go away. More like a zombie apocalypse would have been welcome instead of what we went through. Agents died, covers were exposed, and some of us were left out to dry on our own."

What the fuck?

"Who left you out to dry?" Anger vibrated through him.

"Doesn't matter."

"Was it Robert?"

"No."

He held her gaze, desperate to confirm she spoke the truth.

"Him I met after Caro came into my life. And it turned out he was part of the group who had left me to fend for myself. Who burned me."

"You said he *wasn't* the one."

She shrugged without a shred of remorse. "He wasn't the only one. But part of it, yes." Jasmine fell silent and he didn't doubt she was figuring out how much to tell him. He wanted to demand she spill all of it, but one simply didn't force Jasmine to do something she didn't wish to.

Shit was clicking in his head. "So when I met you that first time, you had no one. You weren't really a junkie, but a Fed who'd been hung out to dry."

She shook her head, lips pursed, and held her hands up briefly. "I *was* a junkie." Jasmine held his gaze without flinching, without trying to hide. "I'll not make excuses for that time in my life. I fell into the life I'd been a part of for so long but without that anchor, it consumed me. I wasn't strong enough to fight it off until I found Caro." She pushed a hand through her hair. "I was an ex-federal agent who had zero ties to anyone. No history, because all of mine had been wiped aside from what I'd created. I agreed to go into WitSec after testifying so Caro could get back to her life."

"Robert."

She nodded. "I don't trust him. The man's a fucking incompetent asshole. I'm not an agent any longer but I hope to hell you have another backup plan in place."

"What did he do to you?"

Her indecisiveness to tell him wasn't difficult to spot. It took a short time but she shook her head. "No. I'm not willing to use my experiences with the man you are supposed to trust at your back. People can change so perhaps he has. I will *never* trust him, but you have to make up your own mind."

Holy fuck, this woman. After all that man put her through, she still encouraged him to make up his own mind. Personally, he would have burned him to the ground. Lance strode to her, maintaining eye contract.

"So if he's not good anymore, I'll be out there with my ass exposed."

Her fleeting smile pushed heat through his veins.

"Now I wouldn't complain, you've got an awesome ass. But you're not going to be alone. I'll have your back."

Gazes locked, tension high, she waited in silence and the words took longer than usual to slip free.

"Good to know, Jasmine."

Cupping her chin, he held her still as he lowered his mouth to hers. Needing just *one* taste. Even as he did so, Lance knew he lied to himself. One taste of this woman wasn't ever going to be enough for him. More, he always wanted more. Craved her taste to be with him once they were apart.

Somehow he found the chops to break off the kiss that had ratcheted up in intensity immediately. Her eyes, a bit hazy, watched him, and he gave her a small smile, loving the way she reacted to him.

"Tell me the rest."

"You know how it is when an agent is burned. Life isn't easy and I had made a good number of enemies while I was under. So I had battles on my hands. Daily."

Unease made him want to puke. He again forced himself to stay still. All he had to do was listen. Jasmine had lived it.

"I paid off debts, did things I'm not proud of, but I had to survive."

"Why didn't you stay in WitSec?"

She watched him without responding, merely cocked an eyebrow.

He got it. "Carolyn."

"I was horrible to her, stole and set her up to take the fall with Declan. Even got her shot."

He nodded. He'd been there when Caro'd taken a bullet.

He dug his short nails into his palm to keep from reaching for her. "But you were there when it counted."

"I've never had family before. To find out one day after being alone that you have a twin you've never met, it changes everything. At least for me it did." She put some distance between them and pushed her hands in her pockets. "I refused to lose that. WitSec, you know how it is. I wouldn't be able to have any ties to her. I'd never get to see my nephew grow up. I couldn't do that."

"So you live in the shadows? How is that being in her life?"

The punch hurt, he saw it when she flinched. "I don't trust the government. That's what WitSec is. I refuse to give people that much control over me again. Especially a group that can change their mind in an instant and leave me exposed, alone and helpless. They help as long as you have something to barter with but if you are an inconvenience, or they don't like you, you're cut loose."

He understood that but still, it chaffed to think of her having to have been out on her own for this long.

"You're good."

A sexy smirk. "I'm fucking incredible."

"I tailed you."

"And I found out." A shrug. "Here we are."

He closed the distance she'd created and continued backing her up until the wall behind her stopped farther retreat.

"It's not going to be pretty."

"Never expected it to be."

"What happens when this is over?" He pulled her shirt from her pants and inched it up her body.

"I go somewhere else. I suspect you have something waiting for you back where you belong."

He didn't know about that anymore. He'd busted his ass to make detective, sure. But this undercover op had changed a lot of his perspectives. All the dirty cops there were, how justice wasn't blind, and more.

Removing her shirt, he stared at her breasts in the plain white bra she had on. How could one thing be so sexy?

"Maybe." That was the only allowance he would give. "Right now, I think you should ride my cock and tell me what the plan is."

She leaned forward and nipped his lower lip. "I like that idea. Strip."

An order he had no problem following.

* * * *

At the end of their days without Dusan back in their life, they lay together on Lance's bed, Jasmine slumbering against him. Her mouth was by his nipple and each exhale put him in another level of hell. His body ached for her but he also knew she didn't get the best sleep so he left her alone, slowly extracting himself from her body. He carefully drew a pair of workout pants on over his morning wood and walked to his kitchen.

He had started the coffee when the door swung open and he found Dusan along with his two bodyguards standing there.

"You do know there is such a thing as knocking, right?" He walked out of the kitchen and watched as the bodyguards looked down at his cock then back to his face. "We still have this day."

Dusan shrugged. "Plans have changed. Where's your woman?"

"Right here, wondering why the fuck you've busted in here when I've not gotten my cock this morning?" Jasmine's voice pulled their focus.

He glanced to his left and saw her there, sheet tucked under her arms and a gun in one hand. Her hair was a tangled mess that spoke of being loved hard and often, and it made him want to bend her over and let that hot pussy suck him in once more.

Dusan's lips curved up. "You like sex? Maybe my men want a turn."

Anger spit through Lance.

Jasmine snorted. "I'd hate for your son to lose the only smart person in his life." She gestured with the gun. "You tell them to come after me like I'm slut on the auction block and I will put a bullet between your eyes. Then fight them. Either way, you die first."

"I have mentioned to you, Lance, how bloodthirsty your woman is, right?"

Lance moved toward her. "I'm aware. Where are we going?"

"A place you need more clothing than this."

"But casual?"

"Yes, jeans will be fine for you both."

He nodded at Dusan. "Give us ten minutes." He grabbed hand and pulled her back into the bedroom.

Jasmine called out over her shoulder as the door closed behind them, "Make it fifteen!"

Another Try

* * * *

Hot coffee in hand, the scent wafting up to her nose, Jasmine stared at the two men who she'd mentioned were undercovers. One was dead, his throat having been slit. From her experience, there wasn't any doubt he'd suffered hard before they'd finally just killed him.

The one beside him in the grave was alive, barely, and he looked up at all of them. She stared down without a shred of sympathy. This fucker was a pedophile. His proclivity was toward children under five. Didn't matter the sex of the child, he just wanted them young.

"He swore up until he couldn't speak anymore that he wasn't a cop."

She looked away from him to the angry face of Michel, across the grave. The man's face a blotchy red. *Interesting.* Her own face schooled in what many people had referred to as a woman's resting bitch face.

Supposing it was true, she really didn't give a damn about the fucker about to die, nor the baby of a crime syndicate lord who looked ready to cry when a favorite toy was taken away. Holding that angry gaze, she put the cup to her lips and sipped.

"Have you nothing to say?" His furious words spat in her direction made her all the more grateful the grave sat between them, protecting her from his saliva.

"I didn't lay a hand on them, not sure why you're so mad at me."

"You were the one who said they were cops."

Tipping her head to the side, she stretched out her neck, aware that not just Dusan but pretty much everyone gathered there watched her.

"Do you really think your father would take *my* word, one of his men's women — who according to you should have walked in through the back door at your daddy's house to clean, not through the front — over yours and the word of people who had worked for him for far longer than he's known me if he couldn't see the proof himself? Your father's not a stupid man. which is why he didn't let the cops in the door. You did."

"I'm going to fucking kill you."

"You're always welcome to try. All I did was tell the truth, and his digging into them pulled their true selves from hiding. I guess it doesn't matter who they were to you simply because you wanted your dick in them."

Lance settled a hand along her back — a silent warning not to go too far. She didn't want to, but she had a thing about being challenged and threatened. Government dick or crime asshole, it didn't matter, she wasn't a fan.

"Enough." Dusan's voice settled his son. "Kill him. I need to have another talk with Lance and his woman."

She barely refrained from rolling her eyes. He rarely called her by name. Not that she minded, it was just amusing in a way. Women were nothing more than pieces of pussy for him, not good enough to call by names. *How the hell did he deal with his daughters?*

Resting her head against Lance's shoulder, she sipped her coffee as if she were standing along the beach during sunrise, not squirreled away in a forest somewhere over a makeshift hole in the ground — one where two more men were about to become food for the worms. There were looks that passed between Dusan and Michel but the boy never pulled his weapon. She studied each nuance of their expressions, including the disappointed and disgusted one on Dusan's face when he eventually had one of his men pull out a silenced gun and end the life of the creep in the hole.

"You cover him up. Too much of a pussy to do what I told you to, you will bury them then come home. We have to talk. I'm leaving these two with you and taking your two. They will *not* help you with the shoveling and if that means, Michel, you are out here all fucking day, then so be it. It's time for you to learn that there are consequences to your actions."

Dusan snapped his fingers and Michel's two bodyguards immediately left the son and moved to the father. Dusan's two remained like stone statues.

Lance didn't move his arm from around Jasmine, continuing to stroke her arm.

Dusan got about ten feet away before he barked, "Lance, come."

Brushing his lips over her forehead, he stopped the motion on her arm and took up her other hand, the one without the coffee, twining their fingers. The men who'd come with Dusan, his personal guards, remained back there with his son. Michel's men were trailing Dusan.

Silence lingered in the woods as they strode back to the dark SUVs waiting along a path she wouldn't even consider calling a road. Lance held the back door of the second one for her and they climbed in while Dusan got in the front. When the second guy tried to get in on her side, Lance growled low and she patted him on the leg, letting him know not to make an issue of this. She had a feeling they would be scrambling later. Right now having a sleaze sit beside her wasn't a huge thing on the grand scale.

"Do you like music?" Dusan asked the question as he looked over his shoulder.

"Yes." Lance bit off his word.

She nodded when Dusan looked at her but didn't speak, instead continuing to sip her coffee, paying attention to the bodyguard beside her and what he was doing.

His gun was at the small of his back and he wore a backup on his right ankle. Other than that, he wasn't armed. A plus in her favor. Dusan's typical men had shoulder holsters for quick draw even in a car. This guy would bumble first.

They drove an hour and finally got back into the city. Dusan took them to a botanical garden. As they got out, she shared a look with Lance. His confusion matched hers.

Dusan charmed the woman at the front who waved them through. He led the way into a section of the garden that was being renovated. Tall plants in both burlap wrapping and pots waited for whatever was being done here.

"I love it in this place."

Dusan's voice was low and smooth. He crouched down and pushed his hand into the fertile soil and allowed a fistful to filter though his fingers.

All three of the men with them looked on edge. She didn't work for the man so she wasn't sure what was normal for him, but from their looks, this wasn't it.

"You know why I love it here so much?" Dusan looked over each of them individually.

"Because when you kill someone, if you put an endangered plant over it they won't be dug up." The words just slipped from her mouth, and the second they had, she wished she could recall them.

Dusan smiled, his blue eyes crinkling at the corners. In that moment, she saw a handsome, charming businessman, not a ruthless cartel leader who ran a human trafficking ring as *one* of his means of income.

"You and I, Jasmine, could do a lot together." His gaze snapped to Lance. "Hold onto this one or she will be snatched up."

"Don't ever plan on letting her go." Lance wrapped his arm around her again, tucking her into his side.

Dusan rose, brushing off his hands. "She is correct. Out here no one would know if you kill and bury a body. They are so worried about the beautification projects no one thinks to ask why the soil is so fertile."

The lighter-haired one of the duo who typically guarded Michel got shifty feet and couldn't hold still. There was something else in play here.

"You two," the man began with a quick glance down to his hands before he looked back at them. "You are supposed to protect my son."

They nodded.

Jasmine believed she knew where this was going to end and she didn't want to be part of it.

"So explain to me how two of the guys closest to him turned out to be undercover cops." He straightened his suit coat. "The knowledge that such a thing has happened, tells me he has been in danger this entire time." His mouth thinned. "I don't like the fact this was going on under your noses."

Fidgety blond stabbed finger in her and Lance's direction. "He's a cop."

Jasmine tipped her head to look up at Lance, whose expression couldn't be read.

"That's your response?" Dusan shook his head. "I come to you with concerns about the men you allow around *my* son and you point at one of *my* men and call him a cop. Instead of shifting the blame, perhaps you should try to figure out a way to save your ass, because right now, this hole has your name all over it."

The blond blanched. The darker-haired man beside him hadn't moved a bit, his expression stone.

Dusan shook his head. "Kill him."

Before she could figure out if that was to her or Lance, the dark-haired man pulled out his gun and put one right in the blond's head, the silencer muffling the sound. Within seconds, the blond had been pushed into the hole and dirt was being slung over him.

When the four of them walked out there was a newly completed area with some plants that had just been planted.

Jasmine wanted to get out of this hell she'd jumped in. She'd had no feelings for the one who'd just been buried in front of her—for none of them from today—but she did care about Lance, far more than she should. Because of that she couldn't just, well, *wouldn't* just, ghost on him and leave him to fend for himself. Especially since she knew Robert was here. Just being in the same city with the man who'd hung her out to dry meant sleep wasn't going to come easy anymore.

One thing at a time. Let's find a way to get away from the man who is everything you despise in a human.

Chapter Six

Sometimes you fall in love with the most unexpected person at the most unexpected time.

"You'll be there tonight. This is not a request."

Dusan's tone was cold and autocratic. He expected his order to be followed. Of course, the man always expected that.

"Black tie?"

A sniff of distaste. "Of course. Unlike my children, I know the meaning of dressing for your success."

"My woman?"

Lance glanced over his shoulder at the woman in question. Jasmine lay sprawled nude over the queen mattress in the bedroom. A light blanket draped over her, covering her firm ass and part of her lower back. She slept on her stomach, arms bent and beneath the pillow supporting her head. Her skin glowed and he grinned even as his heart thumped in a possessive way, flipping and calling for him to head over to her, hang up the phone and drill his cock as far as he could inside that tight pussy until she couldn't imagine what it was like to not feel him in her.

"Of course she will be with you."

The smooth delivery had him suspicious, more than he already had been. There was something going on that he wanted to shock Lance with. Problem was, with a man like Dusan, that could be anything from ordering him to kill a man, having one shot in front of him or any other myriad of shit that he could demand.

"We'll be there in an hour."

Everything inside him wanted to hang up on the man but he knew better. A poised few seconds before a low grunt and the call was done. He huffed and made sure the phone was off before placing it on the oak bedside table, next to hers where it leaned against the brass base of her lamp.

Sinking to the mattress, he reached out a hand and placed it on the small of her back. Not even a full second later, he found himself looking up the barrel of her sidearm, her gaze sharp and *very* much aware.

Lance hiked an eyebrow. "I left the bed maybe ten minutes ago. Did you already forget me?"

A slow blink but no verbal response to his question. Instead, she rose to a seated position, her full breasts distracting him for a few seconds with their dark nipples that hardened beneath his perusal. He slid his gaze down her toned body, admiring the lean muscles that flexed and moved with her.

Shifting her legs, she moved them to the side he sat on but had them so she could slip off behind him. Didn't stop the flash of her pussy that he definitely ogled. Still silent, she set her weapon on the small table before striding from the room without care she was naked and headed into the bathroom. When the water turned on, he moaned and flopped to his side.

He watched her from below lowered lids as she walked back in the room, a towel tucked above her breasts.

Without a word, she moved by him and bent to grab her phone and gun then padded out on silent feet. The moment she was back in the hallway, he reached down and gripped his dick, squeezing hard trying to push his hunger for her down.

"Fuck." He pushed to his feet and walked out to find her in the kitchen, unwrapping a Hot Pocket type of food.

She held it up and popped an eyebrow. He shook his head, not wanting to eat that. While it heated in the microwave, she got herself a tall glass of cold water.

"Dusan has an event tonight we have been ordered to attend."

He watched her throat move as she swallowed. "Okay." Glass on the countertop, she wiped the back of her hand over her mouth. "What kind of event?"

"Fancy."

The microwave beeped and she turned to it, pulling out the pastry and huffing slightly as she pulled it from the sleeve. He groaned when she took a large bite. Eyes wide and watery, she opened her mouth and fanned a hand before it like that was going to help cool it down.

"Coulda waited a second or three." His deadpan remark was met with a narrowing gaze.

"Hungry." She barely waited before taking another bite. This time the moan of pleasure kicked his cock to high gear.

"I'm going to shower. It's fancy and I have to go back to my place and get a tux."

He pulled one out in the shower, because otherwise it was going to be a hell of a night, then frowned as he stepped out and heard Jasmine talking to someone. Towel around his waist, he peered through the doorway and watched her nod to someone at the front door before she closed it on him.

While his woman had on more than a towel, she wasn't wearing all that much. She walked back toward him, picking up a garment bag on her way.

"What's that?"

"Tom Ford." She brushed by him and hung the garment bag on the doorframe. Facing him, she raked her gaze over him and smirked. "Personally I'd rather you stay in the towel."

Said towel began to lift as his cock swelled.

"I'd prefer you naked and on my dick."

"Pencil me in for later." A wink and she vanished in the bathroom.

He definitely would do that. Once he tugged on a pair of black boxer briefs, he unzipped the bag and whistled low. "Love me some Italian wool."

A sharp onyx black. Satin along the lapel and side stripe, peak lapel, and double vent. The crisp black shirt fit like it had been made for him alone. Bowtie hanging around his neck, he drew up the pants and fastened them as she walked out of the bathroom in a barely there dark silvered gray lingerie set.

"Shit."

Lace. It was lace covering her pussy in the smallest triangle possible. Her breasts were pushed up in some lacy bra that was going to have him hard all night. Her lips turned up as she walked toward him.

"You're looking good, Detective."

"You're fucking sexy as hell." He left the pants undone and prowled toward her, circling her but not actually touching. "You trying to kill me?"

"That would be counterproductive now, wouldn't it? I wouldn't get more of that dick I'm addicted to."

Her Cheshire grin had his dick fighting for escape. Giving in to his need, he gripped that very cock and squeezed, loving how her gaze dropped there.

"It's always for you, baby. *Only* for you."

She quirked an eyebrow. "Better be, because if I find out it's gone in anyone else or been touched by anyone else, I'll fucking feed it to you in pieces."

Lance moved toward her and she locked her knees at the pure predation in his gaze. Fucking panty-melting. Jasmine understood why some women had a thing for men in tuxes. While jeans and a tee were her catnip, there wasn't any denying how this looked on him.

He caged her in, hands on either side over her head, and bent close.

"We are supposed to get moving, baby and you being all dangerously possessive turns me on." A deep breath and he dragged his nose along her neck and up along her face. "Seriously fucking turning me on."

She whimpered as he thrust his thigh between hers, lifting her up on her toes, even in her heels. Her pussy clenched, desperate to have his thick length filling her, stretching her. Lance secured his hand around her throat.

Pulse kicking into high, she licked her lips. He squeezed and she rocked against the granite-hard thigh beneath her.

He lowered his face into hers and held her gaze. "Let's go." Another brief squeeze against the flutter of her pulse before he stepped back, and she nearly moaned at the loss of his touch. Lance helped her into her light jacket and they walked down to his vehicle, hand remaining at the small of her back.

She wasn't sure where they were going and didn't bother asking, it wouldn't matter. They'd been demanded to attend so whether it was in a hotel, Dusan's home, or in some fancy building, she was going to be there.

* * * *

He pulled up to the front of the aquarium and she leaned forward, interest piquing. The valet opened her door and held out his hand. By the time she'd unclicked her seatbelt, Lance had moved around and moved the valet out of his way, so it was Lance's hand she settled her palm against.

"Thank you." She didn't pull away as he tucked her into his side.

"The thought of another's hands on you, baby, makes me feral. Let's try to get through the night without me ripping some dumbass's head off and spitting down his throat, shall we?"

They walked up the steps and beyond the large pillars to step inside. Her breath caught in her throat.

Low lighting, a good majority of it by the lighting in the massive tanks that were lining the room. People mingled and chatted as some danced. Her gaze swept the room, taking in the major players in the city.

"It seems like he's trying to see if someone outs us."

Lance nodded as they walked deeper into the room. "You good?"

She understood. They hadn't gone over all the particulars of why she was where she was at the moment, and given both their lives were on the line, she got his questioning.

"Always. You?"

"Never better." His fingers brushed over the top of her ass before he guided them to the bar.

That's where Dusan found them.

The mafia boss wore a tuxedo as well but in her personal opinion, not as well as Lance wore his. Still, the man cut a sharp figure.

"You came." He sipped from a tumbler as he raked his assessing gaze over her.

"I wasn't aware I had a choice." She faced the bartender. "Moscow Mule please."

The woman gave her a succinct nod and walked off.

"You didn't." Dusan stepped closer.

Lance moved between them, bending over the bar to order himself a beer, then he stepped back and kept her slightly behind him.

"So what is this for?" She gestured around the room. "I'm assuming there's something about a charity, which is why you have all these high rollers in one room.

"Yes, we are saving the whales or something like that."

She accepted her drink with a thankful nod and put the hammered copper mule mug to her lips and enjoyed her first sip.

"You expecting someone to out us as cops or something?" She pushed away from the bar and stepped up to the man, noting how his ever-present bodyguards shifted closer.

"Surely you don't think I wouldn't test all theories. You're an unknown and I have had a man following your man there and I've not seen you, or he hasn't, around." A narrowing of his cold gaze as he took another healthy gulp. "Until recently."

Behind her, she heard the top of Lance's beer bottle get popped off but she didn't look away from Dusan. The man was definitely a predator. Looking for the slightest hint of weakness.

Rolling her shoulders in a slow motion, she took another sip, even though all she wished to do was suck it down and get out from under his intense stare.

"Is this the goateed man who spends his every Wednesday at Red Box, getting a handy from one of the staff, followed by his visit to a married woman on Thursday when you have her husband running errands out of town, and Friday he hovers around a school? I don't even want to think why he would be near an elementary school, but then again, given what your son is into, perhaps I shouldn't be surprised. On the weekends he flits between five women and Monday and Tuesday when he's not technically on duty for you, he's in a whorehouse on Sycamore. Perhaps he's expending too much of his energy fucking a shit ton of men and women to properly do his job. If I've seen him, he damn well should have seen me. Not my fault if he hasn't."

Lance stepped in, arm slipping around her waist. "I want to dance, baby."

He tugged her away from the shark-flat gaze of Dusan and onto the floor.

"I've got my drink in hand," she said lightly.

"Why do you insist on pushing him?" He wrapped her tight to his chest, the chill from the beer bottle in his hand along her spine.

"He asked me a question." Her own drink was at his side but she settled her head against his torso, comforted by the steady beat of his heart.

"We're trying to stop him from getting even more suspicious, Jasmine."

"You say that like it's going to change anything. We're here to see if any of these members of the brass or any of the city council people recognize me or you. More likely me as I am the unknown."

They barely moved as the slow, sensual jazz played around them. His thumb stroked along her skin, heating it where the bottle cooled it.

She enjoyed the slow dance and drank her mule.

"Can we at least try not to get taken out back and literally be turned into food for the fishes? There are sharks here, you know." Lance's gaze tugged at her heart.

He maneuvered them to the edge, where they placed their empty drinks on a tray. The music kicked up a bit and he drew back so he could look her in the eyes. She read the intention in his eyes before he said anything and she smirked.

Jasmine lifted her left eyebrow. "You damn well better come correct if you're about to take me out to tango."

"Baby, haven't you learned it yet? I've got all the moves."

An honest laugh tumbled from her as he spun her around and moved them back out to the floor. For the first time since they'd arrived, she was actually excited about what was coming next.

* * * *

Lance drained the bottle of water before capping it and tossing it into the recycling bin at the end of the bar. He moved the bowtie at his neck slightly and scanned the room for his woman. They'd done two tango dances and he was harder than the floor he stood upon. Nothing about her other than pure sensuality and he wanted it all for himself. Didn't want to share. Didn't want to have to hold back.

When she'd walked out of the room in her black dress he'd been amazed by the beauty, he'd not even considered what a dress with two slits in the front where her legs were would be like during a Latin dance.

Now I know.

He'd been hard since the first few steps of the dance, when twirling her had the fringe flaring and her long, toned brown legs flashing. Having her pressed tight to him, the way her hips rolled and shook hadn't helped his blood pressure. At all.

I need to be buried deep inside her.

Continuing his search, he smiled when he spied her moving down a hallway toward the bathrooms. Lance moved to the outside and worked his way around the room to get to the same hallway.

He reclined against the wall until she exited. Lance raked her with his gaze as she stepped into view. She gave him a soft smile and walked right up to him, hands on his chest as she pressed a small kiss to his chin.

"You okay?" Her question was soft.

He shook his head. "Nope." Capturing her hand, he tugged her with him, down the hall. Despite his longer strides and her wearing heels, she kept up. He drew her into a small room and kicked the door closed behind them.

Mouth on hers the moment it clicked, he devoured her. With his left hand, he flipped the latch on the door, locking it. His right settled where he loved having it, on her throat.

"I need you." Yanked. That's how he could describe it, the words were yanked from his throat. "Fucking hell, Jasmine. Watching you in this dress, dancing with me, seeing the flash of your legs as you press against me, having your calf up on my shoulder." He thrust his hips and rubbed his hardness against her.

"Not arguing with you." She nipped his lip. "You need me, take me."

He freed his cock with his left hand, gave himself two short pumps before knocking her thighs apart and ripping off her thong. A low guttural moan escaped him as he sniffed her ripped panties.

Balling them in his fist, he pressed the satin against her lips. Her eyes were locked on him as she opened without him telling her to do so. Lance pushed them in and used his thumb on her chin to close her mouth. Then he grabbed himself once more and slid the swollen bulbous head between her slick lips, notched himself at her entrance and thrust his hips, driving inside her with a single stroke.

Her scream was muffled by the panties he'd shoved in her mouth but he smirked as his own groan escaped. Sinking inside her pussy was fucking heaven. He squeezed his right hand as he pumped his hips. Pupils blown, she undulated her hips and he needed more.

To be deeper.

To fuck her harder.

To watch her lose her shit like she made him do.

Dipping his left arm under her thigh, he lifted her, opening her more. Her lids fluttered as a low moan poured from her.

"You okay, baby?"

"So fucking good," she groaned. "So. Fucking. Good."

She wasn't lying.

He went harder. Deeper. Faster. Swapping out his grip from his right to his left, he put his right hand down between her legs and pinched her clit.

Jasmine detonated beneath him, her scream rising up even though a lot of the sound was blocked as her pussy tightened on his cock, making him spill inside her, wringing out every single drop it could.

Heart beating like he'd just done a ten-mile run, he rested his forehead against hers. Both of them were breathing hard but his heart twisted over when her lips turned up in a small smile. He tugged the thong from her mouth and shoved the damp material in his tuxedo pants pocket.

"Hi."

Her smile grew. "Hi." It was a throaty whisper that warmed him through to the core.

"You okay?"

She nodded and settled her palms on either side of his face, nails lightly scoring his skin. "Never better. Can we stay here for the rest of the time until it's okay to leave?"

"I would love to say yes, but I know they are going to look for us."

She huffed, still not losing the teasing glint in her expression. "Fine, but I'm going to expect a treat for staying."

He thrust slowly, his cock, thick and hard once more, sliding through their combined wetness. "So spending the night with my cum dripping down your thigh isn't a treat?"

"Probably for you. For me, it's more like a branding."

"Well, no shit, baby. Have you seen the way the men in this place look at you? I want you wearing my name all over so they stop looking."

She gasped when he hit deep and her hips canted, allowing him deeper access. He bent his head and sucked on her neck, planning on doing exactly that. Putting his mark there so everyone knew this woman was taken.

Mine.

She shuddered, coming once more around his dick. He pulled out, eyes on his cock as he did, watching their combined pleasure on his skin and hers. Scooping some off with his fingers, he pushed them back inside her. She didn't argue.

Lance put his fingers to her mouth and she opened and cleaned them off before holding his gaze as she sank to her knees and deep throated him.

"Fucking hell!" He slammed his palms on the door behind her.

She didn't tarry. She cleaned him off and tucked him carefully back in his tuxedo pants and rose smoothly back to her feet.

"Wouldn't want you to mess up that tuxedo." She patted his cheek, reached behind her and unlocked the door.

He didn't move back, which would have allowed her to open the door. No. Instead he pushed closer and kissed her, sweeping his tongue through her mouth, picking up on their combined tastes. "This ass is mine tonight."

"Yes." She panted against his mouth.

"Let's get back out there." He drew her away from the door and together they exited the room, side by side, his hand possessively on her hip and on the side of her that didn't hide the mark he put on her neck.

Damn woman makes me feral.

Chapter Seven

The muzzle tapped three times against his forehead before the heavy sigh came. "I really want to kill you."

Lance nearly tensed as he looked up at Dusan from his seated position as he looked over some spreadsheets about the business. He stared at the man holding the Glock. Ungloved and in his typical suit. While Lance wasn't strapped down in a chair, he was at a distinct disadvantage. His own weapon was tucked in the back of his waistband.

"Not that I have a say in the matter but personally, I'd prefer you didn't. Might I know what it was your son says I did this time?" His breath quickened and he worked to bring it back down.

Normally he would have simply gone along, but now, every fucking second here was one away from Jasmine and a chance he wouldn't make it back to her.

I'm not okay with that.

Generally, he wasn't one who believed in all that mumbo jumbo about destiny and such things but with

Jasmine, he couldn't help but feel this was another try for the both of them. Also, it partially justified in his mind how he'd reacted to her when she'd propositioned him and he had tried his hardest to appear unaffected by the brash woman who by all accounts had been a whore and druggie who used her sister for her own benefit.

He'd felt something that day and he sure as hell felt something for her now.

"He says you met with some of the cops from the benefit yesterday."

Cracking his neck, Lance nodded. "We did. Wasn't that the point of the event? Connections?"

Dusan pushed the muzzle against his forehead once more and scowled. With a heavy sigh, he stepped back and lowered his large body down to a tall-backed blue leather chair.

"What did you discuss?"

"We spoke about snowboarding and Whistler." Lance returned his gaze to his lap as he finished perusing the spreadsheets.

"That's all?"

"Yes." He frowned as he looked over the inventory for the most recent shipment. "Were you expecting it to be something more exciting?" Clicking into another spreadsheet, he typed in the code he was searching for.

"I'm suspicious."

"I have nothing to hide." And he didn't—that's all it had been, talking about winter sports and visiting Whistler. "I do have a question, however." He angled the large computer screen toward his boss. "The count of what was delivered doesn't match what had been ordered and claimed shipped. For this item here." He used a pen tip to point out the order.

It was guns, which were listed as auto parts. Front and rear axle shafts.

Shoving to his feet, Dusan slammed his hands on the desk, the Glock pushed off to the side as he stared at the screen.

"Who the fuck signed for this and claimed all was delivered?"

"Two of your son's men."

He muttered in Russian and Lance waited. "Anything else missing?"

"Not so far." He reached out and took a drink of his iced soda. "To be fair, I'm only halfway through."

"Save it and come with me."

Without a word, Lance shut down the computer and got to his feet. He took another drink before following Dusan out of the office.

Two of his daughters were running through the home and they skidded to a stop when they saw him.

"Papa." The youngest, Agata, was five and she had glossy brown hair in braided pigtails. Her yellow polka-dot dress hovered around her ankles.

"Agata," he rumbled, bending to pick her up and toss her in the air.

Her older sister by two years, Iya, was pale blonde and her hair was yanked back in a single ponytail braid.

"You two should be somewhere else. Where is your nanny?"

Iya shrugged. "Michel had her cornered in the playroom. I didn't want to see him hitting her anymore before he fucked her."

It's sad, her language and his behavior don't surprise me any longer.

He set her down and made his way to the door. "Find your mother."

His men flanked him and Lance trailed them. They piled into his waiting SUV and Lance didn't say a word, just stretched out his legs as they began moving. Ten minutes into the ride, he withdrew his phone and opened his contacts.

My woman was the one he clicked on, and he sent her a short message.

Business is running long, not sure when I'll be home.

"Where did you meet your Jasmine?"

"Running from the cops."

An amused snort escaped the man who had been like ice the years he'd been with him. The few times he'd witnessed the man show something else was around his daughters. But for some reason, he found Jasmine entertaining.

"She is a unique woman."

Lance nodded, thinking this was a basic conversation, talking about his woman. For a moment it wasn't crime boss and lackey going who knew where to do who knew what, just two men in the back of a vehicle.

"I want her to do more for me. She is fast, thinks on her feet and isn't fooled."

Every instinct in him wanted to yell 'fuck no' to the man but Lance swallowed that desire.

"I don't speak for her."

Another chuckle. "I know, I wanted to see if you would try to keep me from talking to her."

The urge to end his life for even thinking that he could be close to Jasmine slammed into Lance. "Like I said, my woman can speak for herself."

"I know, but you should tell her to listen to me and accept the offer. It may be smarter that way."

Anger burned but Lance didn't respond other than a shrug. The rest of the ride passed in silence. When they pulled up at the docks, Lance knew his day was about to get bloody.

Damn it all, I'm ready to be done with this.

Chapter Eight

In the midst of chaos there is also opportunity.
~ Sun Tzu

The television was on low as he walked up from the hallway. Lance didn't think Jasmine was even watching anything, she just stared at the wall. He swiped two beers from the fridge, opened them then continued to the living room where she sat.

Without a word, he sat beside her and offered her one. Jasmine wore one of his shirts and a pair of his boxers. She looked fucking adorable and he wanted to keep her in his clothing. She put the beer bottle right against her crotch as she sat there but didn't look at him.

"What are you thinking about?"

"My nephew."

He'd already swept for bugs so knew this conversation would be fine to have.

"What about him?"

"That I'm missing him growing up. He doesn't know me and I don't know him. Hell, I barely know my sister. My *twin*."

Her agony pulled at his soul. What was left of it anyway. Beer on the table in front of them, he angled his body toward her, making sure he didn't physically touch her. Not that losing themselves in the bliss of the physical was bad, for it wasn't, but he sensed she needed something more right now.

"When was the last time you spoke to any of them?"

She sniffed and his gut wrenched at the sight of one solitary tear making a solemn trek along her skin.

Fuck it.

Lance reached out and swiped it away with the pad of his thumb.

"Jasmine?"

"I spoke to her on Christmas when he was first born. Other than that, it's been nothing but cards."

She ran her hands over her face before pushing them through her hair and exhaling even as she flattened her lips. As she shook her head, slightly, she put the bottle to her lips and drank.

Lance held his tongue as she drained the bottle and put it on the coffee table with a yawn.

"Are you afraid you're going to bring trouble to their door?"

"I know I will. Plus I know her husband isn't a staunch supporter of mine." A wry smile. "Pretty sure I wasn't easy for any of you to keep an eye on." She scrunched her toes. "I know he loves her and that's why I don't comment about his behavior to me. He's worried I'll bring more trouble to their home. As much as I hate it, and that he views me in such a light, I respect it because he's trying to keep my sister safe. *And their son.*"

He tucked some hair behind her ear, wanting to continue watching her features and expressions. The hard shell around his heart cracked at her admission.

"There was more than one occasion where I heard your name accompanied by a few choice words." He shook his head. "How is it Atlanta PD had a file on you but he couldn't find anything on you?"

"It gets wiped."

He shook his head. "But you're not in WitSec anymore. What's the reasoning behind it?"

"They don't want me coming to light. I'm nothing more than a huge shame on the Company. I'm a mistake that shouldn't have happened, and if it comes to be public knowledge, they'll look worse in the country's eye than they already do." A shrug. "So it's best for them to keep me off any and all radars. Well, that's what stories are made from." She readjusted her position then tugged his shirt down over knees. "I'm just a ghost. One they wish they could rid themselves of for all eternity."

While her words were spoken with a hint of sass, he heard it. Buried deep beneath the don't-give-a-fuck attitude. The pain and the longing.

"Come here."

She tilted her head in his direction, one eyebrow up in silent question.

"Don't make everything such a battle, woman. Get over here."

Jasmine shuffled over to him on her knees and his cock jumped in his jeans. Ignoring his libido, he tugged her to his chest and let her curl up against him. It took a bit of wriggling and muttering to herself before she settled into him.

Finally.

Another Try

His arms wrapped around her and his chin on the top of her head, they just lay there on the couch. He held her until her breathing deepened, then he dozed as well.

* * * *

His phone vibrating woke him.

With a yawn, Lance pulled it out and answered in a low voice because she still slept in his arms.

"What?"

"Mr. Jankovic requests your presence."

Translation—the boss is calling, get your ass over here.

"Gonna be a bit. You woke us."

"Just you."

That was it, the call ended.

Lance wasn't liking this feeling at all.

"They want you alone?" She didn't stir from her spot against him and he wasn't in any rush to make it happen.

"Yep." Lance twisted some of her hair in his fingers. "I don't like it."

"I think that's the general idea. I'm a wild card and he wants you off your game, thinking and worrying about me."

I am.

She pushed up and gave a small grin. "Good thing it's just a farce and you know I am more than capable of taking care of myself."

"I know you can." He cupped her cheek. "Doesn't mean I won't still worry."

"I'm going to ghost when you leave. You won't see me. I'll be around."

Immediate refusal leaped to his tongue. She covered his mouth with her hand.

"Not up for argument. You wanted me to help you. I'm helping, but I'm also not stupid enough to remain in this place like a sitting duck."

"You're going to piss him off, aren't you?"

That full megawatt smile got him deep in his gut. "Why, it's almost like you know what a troublemaker I can be."

She hopped off him and he grabbed her shirt before she could get all the way out of reach. Jasmine let him reel her back to stand between his legs. Hand on her waist, he tipped his head back to glance up at her.

"I'm going to call you later and you'd better fucking pick up."

Jasmine lowered her head, her black and dark blue hair falling around him like a silk curtain. "You do know I suck at taking orders, right?"

He sought her skin below the cotton shirt. "I know you suck and I love it. But I'm serious, Jasmine." When he reached her warm, soft skin, he breathed more easily. It was just a fact of how things were for him now. Especially with this woman.

"There's not a man alive I will allow to boss me around blindly, Lance. No matter how much I love sucking his dick. There's another around the corner. I do what's best for me. Believe that."

Every single male protective instinct roared to life. On their heels were the possessive ones this woman, and only her, brought out in him. These far surpassed the protective urges he had as a cop toward people.

Rising to his feet with a simple push, he towered over her. Jasmine didn't back down, but held his gaze with a fearless one of her own.

"No other dicks," he growled. "And don't fucking get hurt or in trouble where you need me."

"Listen to me, Lance."

He watched her for a moment, assessing her seriousness, then nodded. "Listening."

"This man will push your weaknesses. You *know* this. You've been a certain way all this time, which allowed you to get into the position you're in. Don't throw that away because he wants to say shit."

"It's not shit when it comes to you."

Her smile could only be explained as sad.

She shook her head once and settled the palm of her hand against his cheek. "Don't ruin an op for pussy. No distractions."

He hated hearing those words from her. Yet it didn't matter. The words she uttered weren't anything that hadn't been drilled into him before he'd taken the undercover op.

That pinch of sorrow never vacated her expression but she nodded and patted his face. "There you are. The man I know will do *whatever* it takes to get his man." Jasmine put her face close to his. "I don't say this often, okay, like haven't ever before, but it's something you need to hear."

Lance refused to release her gaze. Hell, it was going to be hard enough to walk away when this was over. He knew she was only staying to help him in this situation, but his Jasmine didn't feel she deserved happiness. He simply had to change her mind.

"You're one hell of an officer of the law. No matter what you are shown or what you've had to do in order to maintain this cover, you've held onto that integral part of you that makes you, *you*. I've seen a lot of people in this line of work and it's not for everyone. You have what it takes, just don't forget that."

She stood all the way up and moved from his touch. He clenched his fingers around the space where her shirt and skin used to be, displeased with this new situation.

"I'll never say it again, so hold on to that." She winked at him and was gone before he could formulate a fucking word, or process what she'd tossed at him.

* * * *

Jasmine adjusted the wig on her head and smacked her lips at her reflection. The gaudy, bright orange was a hue she would have been okay never putting on once more, but it went with the outfit.

No wonder Carolyn and Declan couldn't stand to be around me. Hell, I'm worried about spending time with myself looking like this. A fucking Wal-Mart reject. Going to end up in one of the memes of what not to wear.

Plumping her boobs in their zebra-striped top, she blew herself a kiss and strutted on. One simply didn't *walk* in clothing like this. You owned it. And strutted. So she did.

Hips swaying far more than she'd done in a while, because the old Atlanta Jasmine had been all about flashy and getting attention, the new California Jasmine was about blending in and not getting killed, she owned the boardwalk as she moved down it, toward the place she knew Dusan and his crew parked their vehicles. People parted like she was Moses commanding the Red Sea and she smirked.

Yeah, she still had it. Even with her horrid taste in clothing, she cut a figure that drew many eyes. And that's what she'd wanted. The clothing was outrageous enough that that's what they would recall. Not her features.

Waggling her eyebrows at two men, she pulled her lower lip between her teeth and dragged a finger down between her breasts as she turned to watch them saunter by. Both whistled and she winked in return before facing her original direction once more.

She moved right by the one who had been tasked with making sure nothing happened to the vehicles. She was never sure why crime bosses felt that was a necessary thing to do. Most people in the area knew who they were and weren't about to piss off a man who would have them killed for even scratching one of his vehicles, much less stealing one.

Then again, they weren't counting on me.

Jasmine had been around long enough and done enough undercover to know that this was going to be a tough day for Lance. Something was going to happen he wouldn't like. Be it a test, them talking about her, or anything else to push him toward the edge, seeing if he would break. How he had gotten tapped for UC work, she didn't know. His moral compass far too solid in her opinion. Then again, people changed.

Look at me.

The men guarding the vehicles there weren't paying attention, again, because, *why* did he need to be? So she wasn't bothered as she walked between them. Without stopping to steal a SUV, although it was tempting, she continued on her way.

After a brief stop, she stepped back out on the street, no longer looking like a Wal-Mart reject, and slipped in the rear entrance to a bar she frequented. A lot. Without so much as a hesitation, she claimed her seat in the back. It gave her an unobstructed view of the door.

She'd spent many hours in here, sometimes sleeping when she wasn't safe anywhere else, sometimes just people watching. Before her was an empty bottle she'd grabbed on her way in. All part of her cover.

She sat there and went over everything. Jasmine didn't trust the FBI. She didn't trust any of the alphabet groups. Any organization that was more concerned with hoarding their own secrets and knowledge than sharing with another company to prevent catastrophes from happening wasn't one that worked with the country's best interest at heart.

"Here you go, babe." A tall glass of ice and a sealed bottle of water appeared by her left hand. Seconds later, an IPA sat there as well.

"Thanks, Corri."

The waitress smiled at her and swiped up the empty. "No worries. Anything else for you right now?"

"This is perfect, thank you." The glass of ice water was what she preferred, because she didn't trust herself to be drinking like she once did.

Two hours she sat there and nursed her water and a beer. One hundred and twenty minutes before her phone rang. She swiped it and put it up to her ear.

"Yeah?"

"Where are you?"

That wasn't Lance's voice.

It was Michel's.

"Donna's Bar on Second. Why?"

"How long have you been there?"

"A few hours. What's going on?"

"Stay there. Father has some men coming to get you."

"Where's Lance?"

"You should be worried about yourself, not your boyfriend." He hung up.

Probably, but she was worried about him as well. Nothing was going to change that.

When the men walked in, she got to her feet and tossed some money down for Corri. With a wave to her, she met the men by the door. They nodded at her and settled in on each side of her as they went up the street.

"Anyone going to clue me in on what's going on?"

Both men, large, with their faces fixed in permanent scowls, glanced at her then looked forward once more. They led her through the crowd to a large black SUV with tinted windows. The driver's one was lowered.

ASPs comfortably stored on her person, she shrugged like she didn't care. However, when they reached the vehicle, she balked. This, once again, drew the focus of both men. The one behind the wheel angled his head to look at her. Then he gazed at the two with her.

"I'm not going until you tell me what's going on."

The largest, his square jaw shaved clean of any and all hair, tensed. "Get in the car."

"Umm, no."

"You need to get in the vehicle. I *will* put you in there."

Her attitude and anger spiked and she didn't think through the wisdom of challenging the man. "You put your hand on me and Lance will kill you, if there's anything left once I beat the shit out of you."

His blue eyes narrowed on her face. A tiny grin turned up the corner of his mouth.

"Mr. Dusan would like a word with you, if you could *please* get in the backseat."

She flashed a grin and hopped in. "Okay." Without asking, she slid to the middle of the bench seat, allowing the two to each claim a spot on her side.

Silently they got in, and the driver pulled out. The low bass on the radio had her bobbing her head along with the music. More than one look came from them. These poor men, they had no idea what she was truly capable of. She had no doubt she could kill all three before any of them were able to defend themselves.

At the agency they may call her a ghost, but her name had been Smoke. She could enter and leave without anyone knowing and she could kill without leaving a trace.

When *Bohemian Rhapsody* came on, she used the seat in front of her as drums, making them feel she was lost in her own world and not paying them or theirs any attention. In reality, nothing was further from the truth.

The moment she realized they weren't taking her to where Dusan was, she knew there would be three more deaths on her hands before the end of this day. Jasmine continued bobbing her head as she reached up and pulled out her hair sticks and used them as some air drums.

Spinning them in her hands, she stuck fast and without compunction at the men to either side of her, driving the sticks into the sides of their necks, opening their carotids. As they died, she lunged forward and snapped the neck of the driver. His death was faster and more humane than the deaths of the other two. Holding the wheel, she yanked him from behind the wheel and got them off the road.

Another check of the men and she hissed in frustration. She didn't want to be in this life again. Now she had to dispose of them. Driving to a place she knew the dead bodies would fit right in, she cleaned out their pockets, then took their phones and other jewelry. Without a shred of sympathy, she kicked the bodies out of the SUV to land in a pile. Then she got back in the driver's seat and headed to Dusan's.

The windows were tinted on this, so she was protected as the driver. And there must have been something on the car, or they recognized it to simply wave her through the manned gate. She didn't have to slow down or anything.

The long drive didn't help keep her mind from racing. Something was happening, she simply needed to figure it out sooner rather than later. And unfortunately, since she was supposed to have been killed, sooner had arrived.

So has later. Where I get payback.

Chapter Nine

It is not in the stars to hold our destiny but in ourselves. ~ Shakespeare

Lance spit out the blood pooling in his mouth as he sat with his wrists tied to a metal chair in a cement room he wouldn't call more than a bunker. It wasn't poorly lit, no, there were plenty of lights for the men gathered to witness the damage being done to his body. He blinked away the drops of blood running into his eye but never once lowered his gaze from the bastard he was going to end when he got up from here. Probably located right now in some damn warehouse.

Michel stood back far enough that the blood splatter didn't hit him. There was a sinister gleam in his watery eyes.

"Scared to get your hands dirty, boy?" Lance tossed an evil smirk at him.

The mob boss' son sneered at him and stepped toward him. "Fuck you, I'm not fucking scared of a damn thing." He wiped his hand beneath his nose. "Least of all a clinger who's trying his best to get close to my old man by sucking his dick."

Lance snorted and struggled to hide his wince of pain. "Don't be jealous. Your old man doesn't strike me as picky, I'm sure he'll let you fall to your knees and let him hit the back of your throat." Lance spit a bloody stream in his direction. "But hey, you move children. Perhaps like you, he can't get it up unless they're underage and scared out of their fucking minds."

Red swept over Michel's features. Sputtering, he lunged at Lance, only to be pulled up short by one of the men with him.

"Get your fucking hands off me. I don't care if my dad says I can't touch him."

His help released him.

Mistake. Big mistake. While they were punching him without abandon, he'd gotten his hands loose from the ropes securing him. Boy Scouts they weren't. Michel puffed out his chest as he once again stood on his own.

He made two fake lunges, obvious frustration mounting when he got no response from Lance. Michel spit at him and rushed toward him. Lance didn't try to avoid him or anything. He allowed the spoiled boy playing at a man's game to take him and the chair to the floor.

Just what he had hoped for.

Slammed into the concrete floor, he winced as the metal slats on the chair's back pressed deeper into him. Michel wasn't a small man, so his weight was substantial. He thrust up with his shoulder enough that Michel grunted and moved.

"Fucker," he snarled. Beefy thighs straddled his chest and the leer grew disgusting. Michel grabbed his dick as he sat there. "I could make you suck this."

"And we're back to you needing to try to get hard by going after someone who doesn't want you." Lance narrowed his gaze back. "Go ahead, big boy. Try it. Take your dick out and see if you can make me suck it."

Lance wriggled his fingers and slid his hand along the metal of the chair, it moved more easily than it should because of the blood on the floor from his body. Michel had locked on him, Lance counted on it.

Michel wasn't thinking how foolish he was being, wasn't considering his father had told him to keep his hands off Lance. All he knew was he'd been slighted in front of his men and his little boy feelings were hurt. He wanted to prove himself out to be far more scary than he was.

"I'm going to make you choke on it." He reached for his pants and undid the top button.

Lance blinked and shrugged best he could. "I'm not impressed and I'll not be sucking your cock. Today or ever. Daddy's not going to be happy with you, boy."

Rage flushed his cheeks a deeper shade of red and Lance snickered. Michel released his pants and swung. "I'll fucking kill you. I'm not scared of you or my father!"

His fist connected with Lance's jaw and rocked him. Okay, that one hurt like a bitch. Michel's maniacal laugh told him two things. One, the man wasn't thinking about his dick any longer and two, this was going to hurt.

Lance took two more punches to the face before he surged up, freeing his arms from behind him and delivering two quick jabs, one to the man's groin and the second to his throat.

Michel didn't know which to grab for, his dick or his throat. And his men weren't exactly fast on the response time. They were more the hired guns you found on a television show. Big, beefy and dumber than a box of rocks. Not knowing how to react without guidance.

Something Lance could and would use to his advantage. They'd been so confident they'd not tied his legs to the chair, so he got to his feet and grabbed Michel around the neck.

"Guns down or I snap his neck."

Part of him, the angry part, hoped they wouldn't so he could follow through on his threat. When they did, he directed them to kick them away, as well as the knives they carried. He'd made it part of his job to know what they carried and when, so he knew there weren't additional backup pieces on their ankles like any good bodyguard would have. They thought they could get away with bullying most people.

Circling, they did a little dance until he made it to the door. It was open—another sign of their arrogance.

"One last thing. I'm going to need you both to strip."

"What the fuck?" The men were more indignant now than when he'd demanded they give up their sidearms.

Explains so much.

Tightening his grip around Michel's neck, Lance cocked an eyebrow. "Really want to challenge me here?"

"Do as he fucking says," Michel spat. "You're going to fucking die for this, man."

"We all have to go sometime." He didn't loosen his hold, nor did he take his gaze from the bodyguards currently in various stages of undress. They stripped down to their boxers.

"Toss 'em here."

More grumbling but they listened, apparently understanding he wasn't joking about hurting their boss. Head canted to the left, he kicked the clothing outside behind him and Michel.

"I *could* let it go like this, but you fucking pissed me off. Boxers too. Toss them over. Although, I have to say, I love the little lightning bolts on yours." Muttered curses as they stood naked and kicked the boxers at him. Their large hands hovered to cover their tiny junk. "Shameful, it's a bit like false advertising. Think you're overselling it a bit. The fact you only need one hand to cover yourself doesn't exactly go promising lightning bolts to your partners. She, or he, no judgement, deserves more."

Lance took the boxers out of the room with his foot and stepped through, Michel still trapped and swearing.

"You boys play nice now." He kicked the metal door shut and locked it from the outside. Seconds later, he slammed Michel up against the side. "How's about you and me go pay your old man a visit?"

Fear leaked into Michel's gaze but Lance didn't pay it any mind. He coldcocked Michel and at the last minute caught him from sliding to the floor. He wasn't gentle about moving him from the building they'd brought him to and tossing him in the back of the SUV waiting out front. In a few moments, he had him trussed up like a Christmas pig and was slipping behind the wheel.

Wiping away the blood that continued dripping down his face so he could see better, Lance huffed a few shallow breaths to try to get back in control. His vision was blurry and he was fairly confident he had a few busted ribs.

He glanced at his reflection in the rearview and shrugged. The blood wouldn't stop and right now, he didn't have time to deal with it. He needed to get to his boss before the man's dick son woke.

"I need a fucking vacation." He pushed the start button and opened the center console. The wad of napkins didn't shock him, he had never seen Michel without food close to his mouth. Hence the need for numerous napkins.

Placing some to the gash, he shrugged as they stuck to the open wound on his head. Putting the car in gear, he drove away from the warehouse district he had been in. As he got onto the interstate, he flicked the bloodied napkin away and reached for more, covering the open injury once again.

The sun glinted down on the road and cars ahead of him, making him squint and wish for his sunglasses. Hell, he wished for a dark room and a bed. And Jasmine.

* * * *

Jasmine crossed her legs and cocked an eyebrow at the man facing her behind the large, dark-wood desk. This wasn't anything new to her, men trying to intimidate her. Especially ones of his ilk, used to women kowtowing before him, scared of his status or impressed by his money.

She was neither. Cautious? Sure. But she'd been across from men far worse than him. It was basically a standoff. Who would flinch first? Who would break?

Not her.

And it wasn't. Fifteen minutes of simply sitting there until a knock at the door pulled Dusan's attention from her. He scowled.

"Enter."

The door opened, but she continued facing the man. "What is it? I'm busy here."

"We found the other men, boss."

"And?" Dusan leaned back in his chair, eyes shifting between her and the one at the door.

She allowed what she knew to be a viperous smile to turn up her lips. "If you're talking about the men who were supposed to come get me to do something, I killed them."

Shark eyes, that's what this man's were like. Cold. Predatory. And they sliced over to her as his expression chilled further.

"You killed my men?" He waved a hand and she listened to the click of the door. It was once again her and him.

"They had it in their mind to kill me and perhaps do other things. I wasn't on board with that." She uncrossed and recrossed her denim-clad legs. "I don't like games. At all. And I protect myself fully and without apology."

"Why were they bringing you here?"

She shrugged, noticing him dip his gaze to her chest. "Can't tell you that. I got a call from your child, who said some men were bringing me to you."

Bushy brows converged. "My son?"

Jasmine blinked, not saying anything more. Most often people filled in the blanks themselves and she didn't have to supply any more.

"That stupid fuck." He mashed a button on his phone. "Get me my son." A deep breath. "Now!"

A scuffle outside the door before a thump against the thick, oak door had her turning in her chair just in time to watch Lance come through the door. Beaten. Bloody. Still sexy. And pissed-off as hell.

Instant rage on his behalf pulsed like a live being through her body. *Someone is fucking going to pay.* Jasmine understood how some people said they would burn the world down for another. Right then, she completely got that.

Lance's angry gaze found her and she was up out of her seat and moving before he had to say a word. Eyes searching his face, she touched near his bleeding head injury but not actually on it.

"Who do I kill?" She turned back to Dusan as she asked the question, her hand staying on Lance's chest.

"I've done nothing but be loyal to you," Lance said, words slightly slurred.

Jasmine moved beside him, angling her body to see both Dusan and the door, where his men had regathered. Once they pulled themselves up off the floor.

"Did the shit work you asked. Helped you. And this is the thanks I get. Keep the fucking position, I'm done. Your fucking son did this to me. Because he was all butthurt that my girl isn't falling over for him and she refused him." He brushed his lips over her forehead. "You okay?" The question was a whispered caress.

"Uh-huh." She matched his low tone.

"Let's go," he said more loudly.

She moved him to the door and Dusan got to his feet. "Wait."

"Fuck you. If this is how you treat people who follow you, nope, find someone else." He stumbled, and she used more of her strength to hold him up, to ensure they didn't give away exactly how weak he was at the moment.

"I said wait!" Dusan's thick Slavic accent made the word difficult to understand, however his tone ensured the command was crystal clear.

Two of his men blocked their way.

"Hold on a minute, baby," Jasmine said. The moment she released Lance, she was on them, taking them down with feral accuracy, her body in destroy and protect mode. And Lance was the one she was protecting. She would burn everything down to ensure success. She secured their weapons and a set of keys. "Arm around me." She positioned herself by Lance again, in a manner where she still had clean lines of shot.

"You *will* let me talk." Dusan moved around his desk, face angry.

She narrowed her gaze and pinned him with an unflinching look overflowing with rage. "I don't care to hear a single fucking thing you say. I'm taking my man to get looked at. You'd better fucking hope he comes out of this without any damage, because if he doesn't, what I did to that bunch of men your son sent to kill me will look like child's play." Her words were cold, bitter, and full of lethality.

He paused, a perverse smile turning up his lips. "I believe you."

"My life is fucking complete now, hearing that. I'm also taking one of your cars and the cops won't be called."

Sick admiration flitted over his expression. "Never." He crossed his arms and rested his ass against his desk. "I'll be seeing you soon."

There was no point in hiding their destination, as the men knew where both of them lived. So she took the SUV she'd confiscated to get to Dusan's and loaded a nearly unconscious Lance into the backseat. Once she had him situated, she dove behind the wheel and got moving.

At his place, she peered at him over the seats and frowned. He really didn't look good. A moment had her thinking of reaching out to his handler but that was squashed.

No doubt we've been followed. And most likely there are more bugs in this place.

Joining him in the back, she straddled Lance on the seat and put her face in his.

"Wake up, Lance."

It took a few tries before those blue-green eyes, hazy with pain, opened to somewhat focus on her.

"My woman on top of me. A dream come true but I'm sorry, baby, I don't think I can do the work this time. If you need to use me, I'll happily lay here and let you get off on my dick."

"Not right now, thanks. I need to get you inside."

His lips pursed. "Isn't that what I just said?"

A small chuckle of relief slipped free. "I meant inside your apartment. Think you can make it to the elevator?"

"Do I get a naked massage?"

She slid off him and reached out a hand to help him up so they could get out of the vehicle. He took it, hand clammy, and more anger surged at what they'd done to him. Michel was going to die.

"Baby, you get inside, I'll give you whatever you want. Right now, I need you to slide forward and join me on the ground *outside* the vehicle."

"Fuck." He groaned. "Thought I'd already gotten out." Lance pushed up, shaky and definitely fading fast.

Taking most of his weight, she walked them inside to the elevator. He sagged against the silver wall as it moved up to his floor. When the car opened and they stepped out, she checked to make sure none of his blood had been left on the wall. Seeing a bit, she wiped it off with the hem of her shirt.

Wasn't perfect, but she could get it later. Not like a lot of people would notice.

Twenty minutes later, she'd given him some ibuprofen, cleaned up the worst of his external injuries and had him sleeping naked in bed. She wiped up the elevator wall as well then returned to the apartment. He hadn't moved, and she checked the bandage job once more before clearing the bugs from the apartment.

Peeking in the bedroom, she made sure Lance was still hanging on to the mortal realm. She finally allowed herself a deep breath. He was okay, she was alive. While she longed for a shower, she wasn't about to leave him alone, so she settled into the oversized chair in the corner, placing her sidearm on the armrest. On the compact table beside her was a small unopened bottle of water. The room was almost completely dark, she could see the door but was hidden unless someone was definitely searching for her specifically. There were pre-emptive notifications set if…when…someone broke in.

Chapter Ten

Appear weak when you are strong, and strong when you are weak. ~ Sun Tzu

He woke to silence. Lance knew if he moved it would hurt like hell. The past few things he could remember streamed through his mind far too fast for him to make sense of what had happened for him to feel like such a pile of shit. Breathing hurt. Even thinking about moving hurt. Still, he opened his eyes for a moment and recognized his room in his apartment. In his bed.

He tried thoughts again and failed. Again. Taking slow breaths, not showing he was awake, he thought about what he could recall.

Jasmine.

Painful or not, his cock responded to simply thinking of her. Where was she? Was she okay? He needed to know he could move when the time came. Lance had to protect her. Other things may not make sense right now, but that, *that* was paramount.

Why the fuck am I in so much pain?

The sound of glass crunching filtered back from the front of his apartment. He flexed his hand and froze when the grooved rubber of a sidearm was beneath his fingertips. A familiar scent pushed through his worry and settled him. He knew that smell. It belonged to one woman.

Jasmine.

She was here. Together, they would figure it all out. And survive.

That was non-negotiable because he wasn't anywhere close to being done with this woman yet.

Hushed whispers came in Croatian and he curled his fingers around the gun's grip best he could. A shadow filled the doorway before moving forward. The lead person of the ones there halted as the silence was split by a single growled word.

"*Stati.*"

The men listened and he opened his eyes to find Jasmine slowly coming closer from where she'd been hidden in the corner, not one but two pistols leveled. One at each man.

"Dusan wanted us to make sure he was okay." Leader Man held his empty hands out to his sides.

Lance struggled to a seated position. One glance to the woman he was fast falling for and he knew this was seconds away from going sideways. Pure fury flickered in her expressive eyes. To him. He doubted they knew their lives were forfeit.

"So that means you break into an apartment without announcing yourself?" She gestured with the gun. "Back up. I want you out of this room. Don't piss me off between here and the living room and I may think harder about killing both of you."

The men complied and Lance swung his legs over the side of the bed.

"You stay put," she growled without taking her attention off the other two.

"No can do, baby. I don't like men near you."

One shifted slightly to the left and Jasmine fired a round right into his kneecap. He went down with a howl.

"That was the one warning shot. Neither of you get another."

"Bitch. You shot me."

Lance reached for her shirt but only grasped air as she slid right up to the man and put the muzzle to his forehead. He whimpered and Lance swallowed. He didn't want to clean up more blood. Hell, he'd lost enough himself that would have to be cleaned.

A coldness emanated from Jasmine, one he'd seen when they had been in Atlanta and she had been the heartless, drug-dealing crazy woman who'd made him want to punch something. More pieces clicked into place when it came to the mystery of Jasmine. Lance began to understand how truly good she was at blending in and not being seen, even while she stood out in such outrageous fashion.

She dipped her head closer to the man, the weapon trained on the other goon never once wavering, and murmured something to him. Lance couldn't hear well enough to make it out but he was fairly certain whatever she whispered to him was in Croatian.

The other man tossed his sidearm away and held out his hands before slowly approaching the one she'd shot. He wouldn't meet her gaze as he hefted up his partner and helped him back out of the bedroom.

No sounds came from Jasmine as she followed them. Lance heard more crunching of glass on the floor but nothing from her. Not a single step. By the time he struggled out to the living room, it was empty. Shards of broken glass littered a few places in his apartment — the hallway, under the window.

He smirked. She was damn good. His amusement fell away as he didn't like her being away from him. *Especially with me feeling like shit.*

A sound from his kitchen and he turned to see Dusan there. Fear sliced through him and he lifted his Glock. But the man didn't move from the chair. In fact, he seemed a bit ashen.

"What are you doing here?"

"Waiting for your psycho woman to get back and disarm the fucking bomb on my chair."

Lance's phone rang and he picked it up from the shelf he was beside. At the table, Dusan stiffened and watched him with wide eyes.

"Yeah?"

"Get some clothing on and leave. Tell that fucker that once you're in the clear, I'll disarm it. Not until then. Get down here and find a white Honda Pilot. Passenger side rear. Let the man take you to a safe house. I'll meet you there." She delivered the words, brisk and emotionless. Jasmine clicked off.

Lance longed to argue but his body was fading and he recognized he didn't have a lot of time before he went down like that man she'd shot in the kneecap.

"Guess I'm leaving. She did say she would be up to disarm it once I was out of here."

"You made an enemy today." The man narrowed his gaze.

"I'm not the one who tried to have me killed today."

"That wasn't me!" Dusan slammed a meaty hand on the table, only to freeze when beeping filled the air. "I trusted…trust you, Lance."

"Didn't seem that way when your own son tried to rape and kill me."

"My son." He shook his head. "Is not right, up there. I have given him too much leniency. This will change."

Lance watched the sweat bead and roll down his temple. Without a word, he hobbled back to his bedroom and dressed in gray sweats, tugging on an oversized hoodie. Pulling his go bag from the closet, he left the apartment. He had no clue where he was going but as much as he didn't trust Dusan, he fully trusted Jasmine.

He walked out on the man bellowing his name. No sign of Jasmine out here but he immediately spotted the white Pilot and slowly got in the back. The Black man at the wheel didn't say a word, just flicked dark eyes to him in the rearview before putting the vehicle in gear and driving off.

Ten minutes in and he grimaced as he shifted toward the door and flexed the hand on his weapon. "Where are you taking me?'

Emotionless eyes met his for maybe half a second before returning to the road. No answer forthcoming.

They drove down into a parking garage and Lance's eyes struggled to stay open. Yeah, he hadn't healed up enough. The vehicle stopped and the door opposite him opened and he lifted his hand in time to see another man sliding a body that looked eerily similar to himself into the seat.

His side opened and he nearly fell. "What the fuck is happening?"

A woman stood there, tall and built like she should be a starter in the NFL. She was stunning, however, and she canted her head to the left. "Walking on your own, handsome, or do I have to put hands on you?"

Lance skimmed his gaze over her, taking in the orange-red hair drawn back in a ponytail. Metal studs lined her face and she cocked an eyebrow. "Looks like I'm carrying you."

Damn if she didn't simply scoop him out of the seat and walk the ten paces to where another SUV sat idling, back door open. She put him on the seat and followed him in, drawing the door shut after her.

"Move."

As she spoke, she reached down to a bag at her feet and pulled out a syringe. Lance wasn't mobile enough to deflect the poke and as his eyes grew heavy, well, heavier, he glanced to the front and found the man he would have sworn had been driving the Pilot.

"What the fuck is going on?"

"My girl put in a rescue for you. Settle back, man. We got this. You're safe."

Head lolling back, he struggled valiantly to stay awake. "Jasmine?"

"The beauty will be along in due time." A dry chuckle. "Don' worry your pretty head over her."

He could no longer fight the results of the beating combined with whatever he'd been given with the syringe. Eyes closing, he swallowed.

"She's mine. You…you don't get her."

That same low laugh, oddly comforting and disturbing at the same time. "You can't hold onto smoke, it always slips through your fingers."

Didn't he know it. "Mine."

He hoped to God he'd wake up again and she would be there.

* * * *

Jasmine sat at a picnic table and took photos with her phone of two men meeting and doing their best to look as if they were doing anything but. She didn't know either of them personally but knew enough to comprehend that one worked for the government and the other had his toes dipped well into the underground world.

They shouldn't be meeting.

Especially not in such a manner.

Children ran around, mothers sat and gossiped with friends, nannies too, watching over their charges. Dogs barked, some kids cried and more laughed. On the surface, it was the picture of idealistic life.

Not anything I would have assumed ever having for myself. At least not until she'd gotten to know her twin sister, Caroline. Her heart twisted at the thought of not being able to see her nephew again, or her sister. No, things weren't great between them, but it was hard to get close to your only sibling when you couldn't risk talking to her or she would be in danger.

She shook her head. Thoughts for another time.

When the meeting broke up for those two men, she waited another twenty minutes and continued acting as if she were taking selfies still before she got up and blended into the crowd moving along the street by the park.

In Chinatown, she walked slowly, looking for the storefront she knew would have the person she sought. Not that she wanted to see him, like *ever*, but it was for Lance, and she'd swiftly discovered for that man, she was willing to walk back into the lion's den.

There.

Lian's Red House of Lion Noodles. That was it, what she wanted. Some things never changed.

Tugging her dusky rose shirt down over her jeans, she walked to the door, took a deep breath and drew the door open. The fragrant scents of Asian cuisine swarmed her and her belly rumbled immediately. Even as she skimmed her gaze over the patrons, she was creating a list of definite "to gets" before she left.

Later.

Right now, something else was more important. She moved through the seating until she reached the table and the person she sought. Jasmine didn't wait for an invitation, merely slid her ass over the opposite chair so she could face him.

Blue eyes snapped up to her and filled with anger and loathing. Robert Gibson.

"You." One word, which dripped with so much disdain she could have paved a highway from coast to coast with it.

Expression blank, she slipped over into the seat next to him, maintaining a line of sight to the exits in the building.

"Let's cut the small talk." Without being offered, she reached for the shiny black teapot with intricate cherry blossoms painted on it. Not losing his gaze, she flipped a cup and poured it.

Jasmine.

One of her favorites.

"What are you doing here?" His gaze shifted from side to side.

"Worried you're going to be outed for talking to a dead agent?"

Cold blue eyes narrowed on her as he picked up his chopsticks and ate some noodles. "I could shoot you right now and no one would blink."

"That goes both ways, you know. I could shoot you as well." A grin she had no doubt was just this side of feral lifted her lips ever so slightly.

"You wouldn't dare."

Jasmine arched an eyebrow, hiding her smirk when his gaze flickered to the fake multicolored bar in her left eyebrow. Always so determined to gain the upper hand though this man was, he focused on easy-to-fake details.

"Don't presume to know what I would or wouldn't dare to do. After all, you know better than anyone how little I like to be betrayed."

He sucked the noodles into his mouth and glared. "What are you doing here then? Planning on calling the cops and complaining about what happened to you? Need me to do you a favor? Put in a good word for you with Lance to try and get him not to hurt your heart?" The last bit was spoken on a sneer.

"I want nothing from you. I know better than to trust anything that comes out of your mouth. Been down that road and been burned before, I'll happily skip a repeat."

He tapped his chopsticks on the plate. "What the fuck do you want?"

"Lance has been injured. The kid tried to kill him." New anger surged and she struggled to tamp it down.

Robert Gibson faltered a moment but regained his composure within seconds. "You know this how?"

"Because I saw him and sent him to get patched up."

One black eyebrow winged up. "He's at his apartment?"

"Nope. We started there but it was compromised. He's going to need medical attention."

"And you're not being a doting little woman and patching him up yourself?"

"You know me, never been one for bedside manner." She sipped her tea.

"I could have you arrested."

A languid blink. "I don't exist, Robert Gibson. You made sure of that, so be very careful. I didn't play by your rules when I was an agent, what do you think I'll do now if you piss me off?"

"I hate you."

She shuddered. "I'm so damn distraught by that bit of information."

He pulled the empty teacup she set down to himself by the handle, using a chopstick. "There's plenty I can put on you."

"You think I'm scared you have a cup with my print or DNA on it? Again, I don't fucking exist. You can't pin something on a shadow." She rapped two knuckles on the table and rose. "I hope you can remember an address." She rattled off an address and walked out, half expecting him to try to stop her.

No doubt he was on the phone the moment she turned her back to him. Had his hands not both been visible she would have assumed he'd pressed a panic button and sent out some sort of bat signal. But the man had been eating. And he was arrogant.

Didn't matter, she wasn't heading straight to her next destination. Instead she went and got lost in the crowd, doing as she'd been trained to — vanishing into thin air. Hours passed and she made her way carefully to her next destination.

More time passed, and she was about to give up, fearing her hunch hadn't paid off, when a group of men looking like they were simply moving down the street to the building caught her eye.

They were good. She...was better.

Digging into the paper bag she held on her right side, she pulled out a carrot stick and munched on it as she weaved through the crowd and nudged her way between two of them, planting the bug on them. "Excuse me." She moved on down the street, an extra sway in her hips.

A low whistle reached her and she grinned, turning around, holding another carrot in her hand and putting it up to her lips as she walked. With a waggle of her eyebrows and a wink, she pivoted again and sauntered off.

Once around the corner, she dropped the sack of food off at the feet of an unhoused young woman without slowing her gait and continued on, touching the earbud she wore.

"I heard he was here. That's what the intel we were given was. Fourth floor. He's injured but don't underestimate him."

Jasmine snarled at the deep, raspy voice. *I knew it. I knew that bastard would sell him out.*

"Why don't we just let him die?" The door was squeaky but soon came the sound of men heading up stairs. "If he was that injured, shouldn't he be succumbing to his injuries? He said she didn't take him to a hospital."

It took every ounce of the training that had been drilled into her to hold onto in any circumstance to keep moving in the same direction as opposed to spinning around and heading back there to take them all out. Slowing her breathing, she stopped at a small streetside café. She stood in line, continuing to listen.

"This floor." The deepest of the voices she'd heard thus far spoke up. "Fifth door on the right." A pause. "Don't fuck this up or I will kill you myself. This is an easy in and out."

Jasmine gestured to a strawberry Danish and set a bottle of cold water on the counter. She slid a ten over the counter and picked up her items before heading to an open table outside.

As she winked at a little girl with blonde pigtails and pink ribbons, she sat and picked at the Danish. The she uncapped the water for a swig. She heard the breach of the apartment door and seconds after that…

The explosion.

Chapter Eleven

*Life always offers you a second chance—
it's called tomorrow.*

Lance winced at the pain moving through him as he shuffled over the smooth floor to the window. Outside the sky was resplendent in purples, oranges and muted golds. He rubbed his chest and squinted out of his one good eye.

He didn't recognize the apartment he was in, and there was nothing to give the slightest hint of who lived here. Perhaps the man who'd been at the wheel?

But then, he thought he'd imagined seeing him with Jasmine. A snarl escaped and he gazed around once more. *Where is that woman of mine?*

His stomach growled and he pivoted away from the window. Lance slowly made his way to the small, neat kitchen. He opened the fridge and frowned. Some tan rectangular containers that were sealed with tin lids and had no writing on the outside to indicate what they may hold.

One in hand, he shut the door to the fridge and nearly dropped the container. Jasmine stood on the other side.

"What the fuck, woman! I could have shot you." His gun was in the back of his waistband and not handy, but still.

The left side of her face quirked up. "Funny." She jutted her chin at the container he held. "Get your food, we need to talk."

While he longed to hold her and kiss her, he used his rapidly waning energy to make it to the microwave and pull the top off the container. Meatloaf and mashed potatoes with broccoli. His mouth watered. Holding onto the counter while it reheated, he watched her in his periphery as she got drinks for each of them.

Were he not half dead and as weak as a newborn kitten, he may have felt it was almost domestic, them sharing the kitchen and working together. His woman wore torn jeans, and through one of the holes on her upper thigh he could make out a tattoo. Eyes narrowing, he licked his lips and moved toward her as she filled her cup with ice. She loved ice. He didn't want very much in his glass but she loved it.

At her side, he trailed his hand down along her hip until he got to the hole and tucked his finger in. "Did you get a tattoo while I was lying here?"

Her smile had his heart skipping a few beats. "I could have had that this whole time."

He clucked his tongue at her. "Not a chance, baby. I've licked every fucking inch of your curves and that," he tugged on the material and frowned, "that raven wasn't there."

She handed him his glass and tapped hers to it. "Maybe, you're just not that observant."

Lance snorted. "Baby, I may miss some things here and there, but not when it comes to you and this body

I've claimed as my own. Trust me when I tell you, I've never been so fucking observant as I am with you."

He leaned closer and flicked his tongue along her lower lip, catching the water droplet teasing him. Jasmine backed up enough to pull their mouths apart.

"Foolish man, eat your food. You're not ready for all this."

He yanked her close, doing his damnedest not to wince over the pain radiating through him at the movement. "Twenty-four-seven, baby. I'm always ready for you."

Her smile, soft and slightly condescending, had him rethinking his statement. She patted him on the cheek. "Let's see how you're doing after you eat some food." She plucked his glass from his hand and carried it to the table. Before he could get back to the microwave she was there, dragging his food from it and taking that to the table as well.

He wanted to snap at her that he wasn't an invalid but damn it all, he kinda was. And despite his words, no way in hell he was ready for tangling in the sheets with this woman. Face-planting on the bed? Sure. But nothing more adventurous than that. Which fucking sucked.

She didn't try to help him to the table, just watched him make his molasses-speed progress. Sweat dotted his forehead and some slid down his back as he lowered himself to the chair. Limbs trembling, he paused reaching for his fork and took several slow breaths. Through it all Jasmine sat there, nursing her ice water. She never once looked impatient or put out by having to wait for him.

He ate slowly, partly because he didn't have the energy to do it any way other than slowly, but also because he was fucking savoring the food. It was delicious.

After cutting a piece of the tender meatloaf, he added a bit of mashed potatoes to the fork with it then held it out to her. Jasmine held his gaze for a moment before she leaned forward and opened her mouth to allow him to slide it between her lips.

"Christ you make eating hot." He focused on her mouth as she chewed and swallowed while sitting in her chair once more.

"And you're still too weak to handle me so focus and eat."

"Where are we?" He took a few moments to cut up the rest of the food and waited for an answer.

"Safe house."

"I don't recognize it."

"Good. You shouldn't. It's one of mine."

He speared a piece of broccoli and pointed the fork at her. With her minute head shake, he ate it and mulled over her words. "One of?"

"Yep."

That was it. Nothing more, no additional information, and he frowned.

"Care to elaborate?"

"Nope."

"Christ, Jasmine. Why not?"

"Nothing more to say. It's a safe house. It's one of mine. End of story."

This woman. "If I had the energy I'd tan that ass of yours for the flippant remarks."

A low chuckle burst from her. "If you had the energy we wouldn't be talking, we'd be fucking, so not exactly concerned there."

He glared as he took another healthy bite of the meatloaf. His focus fell away after he noticed the flare of heat in her gaze as she stared at his mouth. Swallowing, he dragged his tongue along his lower lip, pleased as could be her attraction wasn't fading. Even if she was right, were he feeling better than like shit on the bottom of a shoe, they would be fucking.

Or cuddling.

Talk ceased as he finished cleaning his plate. While it felt incredible to fill his belly, even he couldn't ignore the trembling his body did as he settled the fork down on the empty plate. Hating the weakness owning his limbs, he took his time reaching for his water. Even now, Jasmine didn't say a thing, merely observed.

The cold water slid down his throat and he fought off a yawn, stomach full, body exhausted and needing far more sleep to allow recovery.

As if she knew exactly what he thought, her lips curved up in a slight smile. She didn't speak, merely tipped her head back to the bedroom, and he didn't have the energy to argue with her. He stood and she mimicked him, swiping up his plate and utensils. Lance didn't move and when she turned around from setting things on the counter, he held out a hand.

A slight head shake before she took his hand and grabbed their water glasses with the other. Side by side they retreated down the hall and went to bed.

* * * *

For the second time that day he woke alone. A fresh glass of water with ice cubes rested at the edge of the bedside table. Struggling to a seated position, he rested against the headboard and took a slow drink. Whereas before the sun had illuminated the room, now streetlights held that distinction.

Low voices filtered back to him and he instinctively reached for the sidearm beneath his pillow, grateful it was one, there, and two, not so much work to hold it. One more drink of water and he swung his legs over the side of the bed and headed up the hallway.

He recognized Jasmine's voice, but the other seemed younger. Male, but he couldn't identify it. At the end of the hall, he peered around the corner and snarled with possessiveness. A tall Black man stood close to Jasmine, too fucking close, while on a stool across from them was a young man who looked like he could be a perfect blend of the two.

"Auntie, there's a man lurking at the corner. Mostly naked with a scowl on his face."

"That's Lance and he's grouchy when he first wakes up. Usually because he's hungry."

The young man looked pointedly at him and Lance drew on years of being expressionless to keep the shock from seeing his face show. He was missing his right eye and had a terrible scar down the side of his face. Part of his jaw was also missing.

He stepped into view, nodding at the young man, flicking his gaze dismissively over the man still too close to Jasmine, and walked to her side, where he drew her nearer to him before settling her on the other side. Keeping himself between her and the man.

Jasmine allowed it, and he understood that. She was a formidable woman even when he wasn't recovering. But she didn't fight him on it, simply let it go.

"We should get going." The man had a deep, graveled voice.

"Jazzy said she was going to play the game with me while you talked. You barely talked. This man isn't a problem." The younger one gestured at Lance. "Besides, he came up from the bedroom wearing only his boxers. He and Jazzy are fucking."

A bark of laughter slipped from Lance and everyone glanced in his direction. He shrugged without shame. "What? Kid's right. We *are* fucking."

He flexed his fingers into her side and somehow pulled her tighter against him, turning so he could still keep an eye on the unknown male. Lips to her temple, he gazed over her head to find the man watching with a hint of humor and warning in his dark eyes.

"See. Jazzy, you owe me a game."

"All right, young'un, you seem desperate to get your ass beat." She patted Lance's stomach and moved out from the protective circle of his arms. He stared at her as she shimmied over the floor to where the young man fist pumped the air before he bolted to the couch and leaped the back to land on the cushion.

Lance watched Jasmine do the same thing as the young man and soon they were seated by each other, some racing game pulled up on the television. He swung his focus from them to the adult male still lingering in the small kitchen with him.

"Who the fuck are you?"

The mocking grin didn't ease any concern.

* * * *

The television had some multiplayer shooting game that Den, short for Camden, played. He was playing by himself but didn't seem to be all that put out by the fact. The volume was low, as were the lights. Evening was upon them, and while the boy played in the living room, Lance sat at the table, his left knee pressing into her right. He had been over-the-top protective since he woke. He'd tugged on a dark blue pair of workout pants but had forgone a shirt.

Mark was across from them, the remnants of their dinner scattered on the speckled tabletop between them.

"Where does that leave us?" Lance's question was one on her tongue as well and she shrugged, unsure of what the actual answer would be.

Rocking forward until his chair legs hit the floor, Mark rested large forearms on the table, brushing aside the fast-food wrapper before him. "It's your call, Smoke." A single shoulder rose and fell laconically. "If it were up to me, I'd dump his ass and let him figure it out on his own. You don't owe him anything. Helping him puts you in more danger. I still don't know why you don't just become a PI. You can move around as much as you like, take the cases you want. Do this, what you do now, but get paid well for it and not be in so much danger."

Lance's leg pressed harder against hers but he didn't speak. He watched. Her. Not Mark, who she focused on.

"You know I can't leave him to this on his own. They already almost killed him."

Lance pushed harder. "You both know I'm right here, right? I can hear you. Stop talking about me like I don't know what mess of shit I'm in."

That's the problem, Lance. I don't think you do know what you're in. Not fully. Not completely. And definitely not honestly. His subconscious was right, he didn't know how deep the shit creek he was in ran. Not if he was going to be truthful with himself.

She tore her gaze from Mark's and met the blue-green gaze of her detective. Jasmine missed the icy green of his natural eye color. "I told you about the setup. How they went to the address they thought you were at and would have killed you had you been there. The decision is yours. You want to pursue this and make them pay for trying to have you killed, I'm here to help however you want." She angled toward him a bit more, knee sliding against his thigh. "You want to leave and walk away, I'll help you do that."

"Do you know Robert is in on it?" A shift in his seat. "Like for certain?"

She recognized it in his voice. A thin thread of need to believe that his years of being undercover hadn't been a waste. That this clusterfuck hadn't been but his imagination misinforming him that he had been out on his own, that those he should have expected to protect him were actually a danger.

Jasmine fisted a hand to keep from reaching out to him. "One hundred percent? No. Because his device could have been bugged, I don't know. But he was the last one I talked to and then the men went to kill you."

"You think he is selling me out." A single shoulder shrug. "Or already has sold me out."

"I think people don't change as much as we hope they will." She rotated back toward the table and Mark. "We also know I don't trust Robert. But it's your life, not mine."

He licked his lips and her core clenched in response. In her periphery she watched Mark's mouth quirk. A slow glide of her tongue along her lower lip was her retaliation to Lance before she slumped back in the seat.

"What do you think?" Lance pointed the question to Mark.

Funny, it seemed as if his focus remained on her, however.

"Man, I don't give a flying fuck what you do. I'm here purely because I owe this woman my life." He too, leaned back, one strong arm draping over the frame of the chair. "All that to say, if she says it's wrong and the man is shit, I'd listen to her. I never worked with Robert, but men he worked with, yes. And they were the ones who burned me, nearly cost me my life and that of my boy."

"And your twin?"

Jasmine smiled. She'd wondered how long it would be before Lance brought up thinking he'd seen two of the same man.

Mark shot her a wink and she wasn't positive but damn near that a growl emerged from the man beside her. And he inched closer to her. Jasmine gave Lance about thirty good seconds before his arm was along the back of her chair.

"Don't have one."

"Bullshit," Lance spat.

Oh. She'd been wrong. It wasn't the back of her chair he settled his hand possessively against but the nape of her neck. Strong fingers curving about, his grip familiar and calming.

Damn it! She wasn't supposed to feel anything but lust for him. This comforting and protected feeling she got wasn't part of the plan.

A reminder that had become somewhat of a mantra when it came to this man here. It irritated her to no end that she had to continue remembering that. She scowled. Anger slithered up her spine and she ground her jaw, counting slowly and trying to regain her control.

He leisurely stroked her neck and her insides responded to the familiar touch. It wasn't only the inside either, her skin pebbled and her nipples tightened. A huff of air burst from her lips and she shifted away from him, rising from the chair.

The men glanced up at her but she ignored both of them, walking to the fridge.

"You have water right here, Jasmine."

"Not getting more water, Mark, thanks." She didn't have to turn around to know the bastard had a smirk on his face.

"Babe?"

She scowled at the fridge's interior before swiping a beer she didn't need. Fingers curled around the longneck, she turned back to the table, nudging the door closed with the sole of her foot.

Lance was moving toward her and she sucked a sharp breath. Even recovering, there was no denying his presence. It was simply *there*. His gaze locked on her like a heat-seeking missile and her thighs clenched involuntarily.

Predatory. Hungry. Determined. Possessive.

All words that described the way he watched her. Touched her.

As if he hadn't a care in the world, he backed her into the fridge, arms bracketing her in as his palms slapped the white material of the appliance.

A swift bite to the inside of her lower lip sent enough pain through her to give her a wake-up call. Coldly arching an eyebrow, she waited.

Amusement glided over his expression as he bent his elbows and allowed himself to come closer. His warm breath skated over her lips and she had to force herself not to move nearer and allow them to connect.

"Care to tell me what's got the bee in your bonnet?" A brief pause. "Babe?"

"Just because I wanted a beer doesn't mean there is anything wrong."

He narrowed his eyes and she swallowed, realizing she wanted to see those icy green eyes without the colored contacts in them. Before she could move away, he gripped her throat then moved his thumb along her skin.

Heart kicking up, she watched him as he observed her. Thumb moving to her lower lip, he pressed it in then dragged his digit away.

"Don't hide from me, Jasmine. We're in this together. You and me. The hell with the rest of the world."

If only.

Giving in to her need to touch him, she settled her hand on his cheek. Closing her eyes, she inhaled deeply. The prickly stubble along his jaw abraded her palm and she curved her fingers, moving them so her fingertips slid over his skin.

"This is your life. You need to think carefully about your decision. Do what's best for you, not for anyone else."

He inhaled deeply and brushed their lips together. "My life includes you, Jasmine."

Her heart wrenched and she blinked back tears of desperation and frustration. She was desperate for a man like him, one who would love her unconditionally. Frustration because she wasn't going to have that. It wasn't in her wheelhouse. She wasn't a person anymore. She was a ghost. Not meant to have a normal life.

"Maybe you two can stop playing kissy-face and we can finish this discussion."

Lance nipped her lip, not even bothering to look in Mark's direction at his complaint. "I'd rather kick him out and fuck you in the kitchen. Shove my fingers deep in this pussy of mine. Sink to my knees and lift one of your legs over my shoulder while I lick you to at least five screaming orgasms."

Said pussy clenched with desire. "Five? Aiming high?"

"Guys!"

They ignored him. Lance dragged his nose along her skin. "I can more than deliver, baby. Challenge me again and I'll show you right here. I don't give a fuck who is in this apartment."

She believed him.

Chapter Twelve

Sooner or later we've all got to let go of our past.
~ Dan Brown

Feet tucked beneath her on the couch, Jasmine exhaled slowly as she stared out of the window to the sunny afternoon. Her navy blue, low-riding, fleece wide-leg pants offered warmth that one may think she didn't need on a day like today. But sometimes she merely needed the comfort. Even so, she had tugged on a pale pink form-fitting tank.

It's time for a change. Time to get away from the heat and blazing sun.

Normally she enjoyed it, but right now she could go for something dark and cold to hide away in. Insecurities rising with the speed of the tide, she swallowed back her guilt.

The drugs, using her sister. Her twin. All the other things she'd done in her past after being burned. Part of it was survival, sure, but she couldn't blame all of her behavior on such a thing.

She readjusted her position and tugged her legs up so she could rest her chin on her knees. Arms wrapped around her shins, she closed her eyes.

Time vanished and she sank into her thoughts, the good, the bad, and definitely the ugly.

A hand on her shoulder.

Without hesitation, she reacted. Lunging up and around in a single move, she struck for the throat, meaning to incapacitate as she wasn't carrying. Not a mistake she would make again.

"Holy fuck!"

The male went down stumbling back over his own feet, but it wasn't enough. Touches were bad, they meant things were going to happen to her. She rode him to the floor, landing with a grunt, her legs on either side of his chest, knees bent.

Holding herself over his form, she snarled as she continued to strike.

His mouth moved, but the words blurred and couldn't penetrate the haze surrounding her. It sank in, finally, that he wasn't fighting back. Not trying to harm her, but simply deflect her attacks.

She bared her teeth and went for his eyes. He moved to block and flipped her over, pinning her to the ground. Arms stretched above her head, his heavier weight pinning her hips down.

Bucking hard, try as she might, she couldn't dislodge him. Panic welled up and she refused to give in. Not again.

He smacked her cheek, not overly hard but enough to jar her.

What was happening slammed into her and she lay there beneath Lance, chest heaving as she struggled to ingest the slightest bit of air.

"You with me, Jasmine?"

Sweat dripped down her face, soaked her back and through her tank top. He didn't rush her, just sat there, watching her, eyes locked on her face as he continued to hold her wrists and keep his weight on her pelvis.

She dragged her tongue over her dry lips, shame rose and he clucked his as he shook his head.

"No, baby. Focus on my voice, not on any shame you may think you deserve to feel."

He dipped his head, his dark hair falling forward. No anger existed on his features.

"I'm letting go of your wrists."

He put action to his words and released her. Watching him with suspicion and shame, she brought them to her torso and rubbed. Not because he hurt her, no, merely because she needed to do something with her hands. Lance had been extremely gentle with her given how much she'd been fighting him.

"You with me?"

It was a struggle to even nod but she managed to give him a small one.

"Good girl." Eyes locked on hers, Lance placed his hands by her shoulder and with a swift move lifted himself off her, settling once more at her side.

She didn't hesitate, jumped up herself and beelined it straight to her room. She closed the door behind her, and had made it three steps to her bed when it popped open.

"I don't think so, baby."

"I can't... Leave it alone." She didn't turn back toward him.

Even as the words left her mouth, she knew it wasn't meant to be. Lance Baldwin did his own thing. Forged his own path.

"Not happening, baby."

She felt him near. As always, the comforting warmth that never failed to surrounded her when he was close wrapped her up once more. He skimmed his touch over her bare shoulders and down her arms so he could lace their fingers together.

Shame flooded her and she remained rigid as his larger body curved around her. He shared his heat, his strength, his protection.

"Come on, talk to me."

Coaxing, his words strummed along her skin and tugged at some need she hadn't realized she had within her to share with this man. To allow him to shoulder some of her burden.

Had he been in front of her she would have glared at him. He wasn't.

"My helping you keep your ass alive isn't contingent on you knowing my personal feelings, Lance."

His arms flexed around her and he pressed his lips to the rapid pulse in her neck.

"I'm not letting this go, baby." He moved them to and the bed and put her on the mattress first before climbing in behind her.

She appreciated him not making her face him. "I'm fine. I'll work through it."

"Let me help you."

Four words. Four words that gutted her on every level.

"Why? We're pretending to have a relationship purely to keep you breathing and not becoming a corpse. You don't need to pretend this is anything other than what it is."

He circled her neck with his large hand, tightening his hold.

Fucking hell. She melted, core dampening and clenching for him to fill her. Bad-ass bitch turned wanton hussy the second this man gripped her neck. *Fucking pathetic.*

"Why do you hate yourself so much?"

A humorless laugh burst from her. She reached up and grasped his wrist but didn't attempt to pull him off her, just allowed herself to rub her thumb along his skin.

"I'm not exactly anything to be proud of."

"Bull-fucking-shit." His tone was firm. Absolute. "You're amazing. A fucking survivor."

"I'm also a shit person, Lance. Let's not forget the drugs, lying, stealing, and endangering my family."

"You made a bad decision when all you had were shit ones. You can't continue to beat yourself up over that, Jasmine. Why can't you forgive yourself?"

"Because I used my twin. I barely knew her and honestly, if she'd not been what I needed to get out of the situation I was in, I don't think I would have ever reached out." Shameful tears burned her eyes and a few traitorous ones leaked free.

"I think you would have. Maybe not as soon as you did, but she's your twin, and once you learned about her, nothing would keep you apart for long. If that thought of yours was true, this wouldn't be eating you alive."

She huffed at his words.

"And you showed back up when you'd said you would." He used his hand not on her throat to draw abstract patterns on her exposed belly. "You defended her and threated to pull your testimony unless she was protected, not once worrying about your own safety."

She clenched her jaw and screwed her eyes shut. "And I also fucked the man who ended up betraying her and getting her kidnapped, all because he didn't like being ignored."

"While hearing you talk about men who've been blessed enough to touch this body is at the bottom of my 'Things I love to do' list, *his* behavior isn't yours to control. Stop shouldering the world's problems, baby. You can't save everyone."

She sagged into his chest, his words freeing in a sense. It was different trying to come to this conclusion by herself versus having someone tell her with such definitiveness.

His fingers continued their idyllic motion on her belly. "Why do you think you aren't deserving?" A deep breath. "Of anything good in this world of shit, what did you do that makes you less than every other human?"

"I wasn't always like this."

His breath ghosted her ear and she opened her eyes to stare at the bare, water-stained ceiling and the wall with torn blue-flowered wallpaper. "Baby, I don't think you're like this now, you simply have the mistaken belief you don't deserve better."

She skimmed her short nails up and down his corded forearm, and the demons she'd held inside for years bubbled over.

"She was my best friend. We went through training together. Her nickname was Moonlight."

"Smoke and Moonlight." His squeeze was subtle but she got the message. He was ready to keep listening.

"When the op," she cleared her throat, "our op went sideways, and out of the stratosphere sideways, I wanted to get out, like we should have without question. I wanted to stay and help. Had the misguided belief it was our duty. So we stayed." Nausea churned.

"We had carried two kids out from the burning building that hadn't been cleared despite what had been claimed. Seconds after she handed the child off to the parent, she took one in the head. Her blood and brain matter all over me as I watched my best friend die. They told me it was our fault for trying to be heroes and save the children." A shudder. "She was Mark's woman. Den called her mom, even though she came into their life after he'd been born. Everything I touch, anyone I love, they are in danger. I even attacked you for simply touching my shoulder."

Every tear, every whimper, ripped out what was left of his heart. The devastation in her tone and the pain drowned him. The sun was lowering in the sky, turning the small bedroom a soft golden hue. This room had the general safe-house feel, nothing personal, only practical. But right here and now with this woman beside him, it felt like more.

Or like it could be.

They weren't in a position to think more than their present. And yet, he did. He was. As much as he could, his thoughts were on ways to tie this woman to him in a permanent way.

"I'm fine, Jasmine."

She didn't respond. Her light touch on his arm was grounding him and, he thought in a sense, doing the same for her. She was private. Clammed up. And deadly as hell, but she cared more than she ever wanted people to know, so for her to feel so bad about being alive gutted him.

Without asking for permission, he rotated her so she faced him, allowed her to tuck her face into his neck.

Sprawling his hands along her spine, he nudged her even closer, securing a leg over hers.

"Jasmine."

"Don't, Lance. I'm just… Don't. Please." The words were a bare whisper, exposing all her fragility which she normally hid behind iron doors.

That dried up all his questions in a flash. This woman, the proud, feisty, sexy woman didn't say please. Until now.

"Okay, baby, but we will talk about this later."

Her response wasn't verbal. No, she wrapped her strong arms around him and held tight. Small sobs rocked her and all he could do was take it. Close his eyes, tuck his face in her hair and stroke her back, offering the silent support he hoped would be enough.

This went far deeper than putting her sister in a rough predicament. It was years of not having anyone but herself to count on. Of being let down by those who were in positions of mentorship and power tossing her away as if she were disposable.

"You're enough, Jasmine. Trust me, baby, you're enough."

* * * *

When she walked out into the living room three hours later, he watched her from where he stood over the skillet as he finished up the pan-seared pork chops. The mashed potatoes were done, the sauteed veggies were on the back burner, covered and waiting. He watched her as she strode into the kitchen.

Armor's back in place.

Her hair was piled on top of her head in a messy bun, her sweats hung low on curvy hips and it was his shirt that covered her upper body. That, he approved of.

"Perfect timing." He turned off the stovetop and carried the pan to the table and set it on a cream-colored pot holder.

"What's the occasion?"

Shooting her a glare over his shoulder as he returned to the stove for the veggies, he shook his head. "Nothing other than I thought we deserved to have a nice meal."

She watched a bit before popping her shoulders and grabbing two beers from the fridge.

At the table, Lance served her before himself and kept his thoughts private as they ate. He didn't want to ruin the meal, but she was fucking delusional if she believed he was going to let it go completely.

* * * *

Alternative rock played as they cleaned up, doing dishes shoulder to shoulder. He washed and she rinsed and dried.

"I hear your sighs over there, you know." She flipped the towel over to land on the counter as she faced him. "What do you need to say?"

Lance dropped the sponge in the lukewarm water with minimal suds and gripped the sides of the sink.

"I want to make you sit down and listen to me about how you're not a waste and that you fucking deserve happiness." He'd started his declaration looking at the water but ended staring in her eyes.

"My own brother-in-law doesn't want me around because I'm a danger to my twin sister and his son. The government would lock me away in a dark hole and throw away the key because I'm a reminder of things that went wrong. I've done shit that anyone with a slight sense of right and wrong would find reprehensible."

Rolling his lower lip between his teeth, he reached by her to swipe the towel in order to wipe his hands off on it. He balled it up and set it back on the counter. Lance shook his head and cupped her jaw, narrowing his eyes when she shifted like she was going to pull away.

"Baby, tell me what you've done the past year."

She pushed his hand off and blinked. "What?"

He took a deep breath digging deep to ensure his voice remained calm and modulated. "This past year. Before you ran into me in the alley, what have you done?"

A slight narrowing of her eyes as she thought before responding. "Hunted down some traffickers, put some drug dealers out of business and worked some odd jobs to help out some of the unhoused." She crossed her arms. "Why?"

Lance mimicked her stance. "If you're this horrible person you seem to be fixated on being, what the fuck is that? Where's the stealing vehicles, getting drunk and beating someone to death, the doing drugs? Where's that on your list?"

She narrowed her eyes at him, brow furrowing before she huffed two deep breaths as her expression relaxed, realization settling. "Oh."

"Yeah, baby. Oh." He stepped close and held her face in his hands. "*You* are an amazing woman, you fight for those weaker than you, you risk yourself for those you have no use for, including working with me and Robert, all the while putting your own mental health and well-being on hold to do what's right. Nowhere in that, and I mean fucking *nowhere* in this world does a person who is shit at being human do those things." He wedged a thigh between hers and turned her so the counter was at her back. "You're a good person, Jasmine Hoyer. Fucking incredible. Say it."

She shook her head and he stepped closer.

"Tell me that you're a good person."

A frustrated huff. "I'm a good person." She rolled her eyes but held his gaze.

Completely serious, he nodded. "Yes, you are. And I'm going to remind you of this until you start to believe it yourself."

Chapter Thirteen

Everyone deserves a chance to clean up their mistakes.

Lance watched as Robert strolled into Lian's Red House of Lion Noodles. Anger surged as he thought about everything that had gone down with the attack on where he was supposed to be recovering. Just like Jasmine had said would happen. She'd warned him the man couldn't be trusted and something would go sideways.

The man had not a single care in the world and while he longed to rush in and confront him, Jasmine had also informed him the man usually had a man following him. Just in case.

So he'd waited. It wasn't like he needed her to tell him how to do his job. He'd joined the military the moment he turned eighteen, served four years and became a cop. He'd been a cop for most of his life. He was a detective now and did undercover work. But he'd just been betrayed by a man he should have been able to trust.

As far as he was concerned, his cover had been blown wide open. *Which means I'm burned.*

"What the hell is that woman doing?" Lance scrubbed a hand over his face as he blinked a few times, trying to convince himself he was imagining seeing her there.

Jasmine sauntered into view, tight jeans, hot-pink wedge sandals and a crisscrossed tank top in the same color as her footwear. His cock kicked as he watched her move. Fluid. Sexy. And dangerous as hell.

To more than just my heart.

He'd heard rumors of Smoke when he'd first gone undercover. Honestly, he'd thought it all a bunch of BS that the guys were telling one another. But having known her, seen her in action, he had come to believe it.

Which begged the question, why had she been burned? Why did they turn on her? Someone so dangerous. And why hadn't she gone after them in retaliation?

He shook his head and frowned. Right now, he needed to focus. And part of that focus had to be on his safety, not on the woman who'd just twitched her ass right in the door of the building he wanted her far away from.

Crossing the street, he smiled at the couple at the door before he held it open for them. Soft music greeted him along with mouth-watering, tantalizing scents. The tiny woman at the front picked up a menu and smiled.

He gave her a small nod and pointed. "I see my party."

"Okay." The menu went back to the counter and she put her attention on something else.

Lance walked through the establishment, noticing how most people didn't pay him a lick of attention. Especially the one who he'd come to see. But he also didn't see his delicious woman wrapped in hot pink. Strange, because he didn't think she would be blending in with that color.

Without preamble, he slid into an empty seat across the table from Robert. The man glanced up, his eyes widened and he looked feverishly around.

"Shit, I heard you'd been—" His skin remained pale. "Are you okay? I mean, with what I heard? That you were dead? Been killed."

"I imagine so. The men you sent to do the job didn't want to report failure."

He paled further, shaking his head. "You have to believe me, I didn't set you up." He swallowed. "It had to be Jasmine."

Lance leaned back in his chair, reached for the tiny porcelain cup on the table and spun it in his fingers. "What reason would Jasmine have to kill me?" He lifted a shoulder as if he hadn't a care in the world when, in truth, he had to dig deep to keep himself on the opposite side of the table from Robert. "Had she wanted that accomplished, she simply could have told Dusan I was undercover, blowing my cover instead of helping me out."

Robert's nostrils flared and he clenched his jaw. "I know her. She's dangerous. There is a reason she was blacklisted."

Lance stilled his fingers on the cup. Took a deep breath. A single slow blink. When he opened his eyes, Robert was watching him like he was a caged animal.

Maybe the man wasn't so stupid. But he'd tried to have him killed so…he was.

"I didn't ask."

The man smirked and bent toward him like he was about to impart a huge secret. "But you want to know, don't you?" He dipped an egg roll into some sauce and chewed a bite. The red dipping sauce dripping down his chin. "You put your dick into her and you're wondering what you've done." Robert used the back of his hand to eliminate the excess sauce on his chin.

Fucker was right. He did want to know. Purely because Jasmine had gone tight-lipped on it and wouldn't share a damn thing about what had happened to her. And he couldn't go digging around on her. He wasn't acting as a law enforcement officer at the moment, he had to maintain his cover.

Lance wanted to protect her. Give her what she wanted. Keep her in his life. He knew she was building walls between them. He watched her do it, even as he was dick deep inside the best pussy he'd ever had in his life. It killed him a bit, but he wanted what she was willing to give. When this was over, then he would turn his focus to keeping her.

"You seem to like hearing yourself talk, so go ahead. Tell me. Because you talking is all that's keeping me from doing to you what I really want to do given the group of mercenaries you tried to kill me with."

Robert finished off his egg roll and reached for a potsticker. "She was the top of her field."

"Tell me what I *don't* know, not what I do."

Anger flashed in his blue gaze but Robert obeyed. "Had skills that even our senior members were in awe of. She was cold, calculating, ruthless. Things I'm sure you've seen for yourself."

"I get you food?" A slender young woman stopped beside the table and glanced at Lance.

"No, thank you. How about just a Coke with ice?"

She nodded once and bent to set a napkin on his lap. He gripped her wrist when her hand slid a bit too close to his junk for comfort. Across the table, Robert smirked.

Narrowing his gaze at the man, he jutted his chin. "Keep going."

The waitress brought his drink and set it down before walking away without a word. He reached for the napkin to move it and felt a piece of paper in the cloth.

Robert pulled a big swig from his drink and began talking. Giving him part of his attention, Lance slowly unfolded the sheet of paper and read it.

Your luck ran out.

"And the entire thing went pear-shaped. I didn't plan for her to get blacklisted or burned. I had no" — he slowed — "choice. What? What is it?"

"If you honestly didn't do it, you need to get the fuck out of here now."

Robert sobered up quickly. "What are you talking about?"

"I just got this." Lance slapped the note on the table between them. Didn't speak while the other man took a quick read.

"The fuck?" Robert shifted and looked around before shaking his head. "I don't know. I come here all the time."

"I know." For a man who should be so aware of how not to be predictable, he was dumb to believe that someone couldn't have him pegged.

"I've made this my place to eat."

"I know." Lance swiped the note and shoved it in his pocket.

"I'm like a regular here."

He rolled his eyes. "I *know*."

Robert finally glanced in his direction, concern on his features. "And you still don't think this is Jasmine. Even after all I told you?"

"You're on her shit list. Not me."

The sneer returned. "Right, you're on her fucked list."

"Ing, Robert. Fucking list. She and I ain't done." Truth be told, he wasn't sure they ever would be. "If you claim you didn't set me up and people know I'm here with you because you wouldn't vary your lunch spot, that means you're also in danger." He rubbed the nape of his neck, an itch arriving between his shoulder blades, warning him of impending danger.

"I'm in contact with one person at the bureau. One. They didn't want me to touch base with many people since I was your handler, and if they got to you and found me, shit could happen."

He drank some Coke. Why not. He was already marked. May as well quench his thirst. "As opposed to what's happening now."

Robert leaned over the table. "I told you. I had *nothing* to do with that attack on you."

A dot appeared on Robert's chest. Flashing. Lance scowled and stared harder, doing his best to make out the message in morse code.

"We need to move. Now!" Tossing some bills, he thrust a hand forward. "Out the back, now! Move, move, move!"

Behind them, glass shattered, bullets sprayed, people screamed.

* * * *

Jasmine paced back and forth in front of the safehouse door. Part of her longed to rush in and visually confirm that he was fine. The rest of her wanted to rush in and throttle Robert for being the dumbass he was.

Aware of her hair trigger, she paced. And paced some more. Mark and Den had been advised to stay away, by her, given the unfolding situation. She didn't trust Robert, not as far as she could throw him. She had been in the restaurant, had nearly gutted the woman for daring to lay a hand on Lance, but had controlled that new urge.

She'd been sequestered in a place allowing her a direct line of sight to Robert, where she could eliminate him if it became necessary. *It's always been necessary to wipe him from the face of the earth to me, but for whatever reason, Lance wants to trust him.*

She'd not been lying when she'd said it was his choice. If he wanted to trust the man, that was on him. Not her. Even so, she'd not been able to leave him to his own devices when he'd gone to confront him. Nor warn them both when the hit squad rolled up. Someone must have though, she had an idea of who had, but no proof.

Now I have a man I can't stop thinking about fucking on the other side of the door. And a man who I want to fuck up.

Shaking her head, she slipped down the steps, not ready to face anyone. She wove in and out of the crowd milling along the sidewalks. Cars zoomed by, people yelled back and forth to one another, dogs barked and a mingle of scents filled the air. Some good, many terrible, but all part of living in a city. About two miles away, she slowed before an ice cream parlor. Children laughed and squealed as they ingested far more sugar than they should.

With a smile, she walked through the mass of sticky faces and fingers to place an order. The harried woman behind the counter gave her a tired grin as she scooped up some Rocky Road and put it in a waffle bowl.

"Thank you." Ice cream in hand, she retreated to the outside seating and enjoyed a few bites before she pulled a burner cell from her pocket. Spoon in her mouth, she took a deep breath and punched in the known numbers then held it to her ear.

And waited.

"Hello?"

Her heart clenched at the sound of her twin's voice.

"Hello? Is someone there?"

Jasmine bit her lower lip and reined in her need to respond.

"Okay," Caroline said. Her voice was soft and soothing, just another way they were opposites from each other. "Okay. In case you were wondering, we're fine. He asks about you a lot. We miss you. We *love* you." A sharp breath. "Come home. Please."

Jasmine jabbed her thumb on the button to end the call, the first traitorous tear leaking free. Hand wobbling, she set the phone on the dark gray wrought-iron tabletop. Two more tears dripped down and she jerked, knocking over her ice cream bowl.

"Of course."

"Don't cry, lady. You can get more ice cream."

A small hand settled upon her jean-clad leg and she opened her eyes to find a pair of dark green eyes staring up at her. His blondish brown hair was an unruly mess but he was freaking adorable. Her ovaries exploded.

She gave him a small smile. "You're right, I can." Jasmine righted the bowl that had tipped and tucked the spoon inside as she reached for some napkins to clean up her mess. "Thank you."

"I spill my ice cream all the time. I used to cry but Daddy said we can just get more."

Eyes dashing around the area, she looked for someone who seemed to be in charge of this child. She found him, built like Lance with dark chocolate hair. The man was locked in on the boy and her.

Her insides purred. A dad and his kid, a weak spot for her. "Your daddy sounds like a very smart man."

He took a long lick of his blue treat with the sprinkles and what looked to be cookie dough or cake bites in it. "He is. Even if he only likes boring ice cream." Without being asked, he dragged over a chair and climbed up, mindful of his ice cream. "He likes chocolate." Another lick. "He's over there." The boy jabbed a finger in the direction of the observing male.

She looked again and the man picked up something from the cashier in each hand then walked toward them. Her belly clenched. Who the fuck was this man and why were her lady bits going crazy?

Not as crazy as they did for Lance, but enough she wanted to squirm on the seat. Tight jeans hugged his lower body, black boots stuck out from the bottom. A faded and worn blue shirt only amplified his upper torso's strength. She wasn't the only one looking.

Men and women were checking him out. Some men glowered at their women, some glowered at their men. Women were plumping up their breasts, thrusting back shoulders.

Holy fuck it was hot. She nearly took the kid's ice cream to have something cool.

"Found us a seat, Daddy."

His loose-limbed gait showed off his power. She swallowed as he neared. Green eyes like the boy's met hers. The corner of his mouth twitched up. "Did you ask this beautiful lady if we could join her?"

That voice. Good lord, angels were weeping. Much like parts of her body.

"She was crying. I made her feel better. We're friends now, it's okay." The kid kicked his feet as he ate, seemingly completely content with how things were going.

"Thank you for making her feel better." Another waffle bowl with Rocky Road settled in front of her. "Lady said this is what you had. I saw yours tip over."

"Thank you, but it wasn't necessary."

His smile was sinful. "It was. We're crashing your table. Unless…"

She knew what he wasn't asking. "It's fine." Jasmine moved her dumped ice cream and the napkins to the side and picked up the new spoon he'd delivered along with the bowl.

"Name's Nolan. This is Liam."

It was easier on her overall to look at the boy, who now had a ring of blue around his mouth. "Nice to meet you both. I'm Jasmine."

Liam smacked his lips. "Like a flower. You're pretty like one too, huh, Daddy?"

"You got it, bud."

She put a spoon of ice cream in her mouth and willed her body to cool down. This was freaking insane. She didn't get horny like this. Not with a man she didn't know.

Then again, I did proposition the good detective when I first saw him. Her core clenched at the thought of Lance.

Keeping her head down, she took several slow, deep breaths before lifting her gaze once more.

Nolan watched her, those electric dark green eyes locked onto her face. He winked and her panties damn near combusted. Oh, this man was lethal.

"She could be my new mama."

Jasmine paused with her mouth on the spoon and flicked her glance between the two men at her table.

His smile wasn't gentle, it was rough with the promise of endless pleasure. "I don't think so, bud."

Liam continued kicking his feet. "Why not? You said she was pretty."

"She's beautiful. But she's also taken, based on the frown from the man behind her."

She cocked an eyebrow and drew the spoon from her mouth. "Really?"

He nodded slowly, the rhythmic *thunk* of Liam's shoes on the table steady and oddly calming. "Tall man. Dark hair. Glowering like he's the devil and I've touched his favorite toy."

"You should share, Daddy."

"I'm game for sharing. Are you?" The question was directed at her and she swallowed down her laughter.

"Sorry, not this time." She glanced behind her and frowned when she saw Lance leaning against the fencing post for the outside area. Eyes on her. Locked. *How the fuck did he find me?*

"Very well then." He winked once more and went back to his ice cream. Chocolate double scoop on a regular cone. Not a waffle. "If you change your mind."

"She won't."

Lance gripped the nape of her neck and immediately her body heated like it had been on an ice cube before.

No matter how hot — and he *was* hot — Nolan was, her body was owned by Lance Baldwin.

"We need to get going, baby."

There was something in his tone that had her moving instantly. She held up the newer ice cream. "Taking this for the road. Liam, it was a pleasure meeting you. Thank you for cheering me up."

He grinned at her, unaware or uncaring of the undercurrent of tension streaking between the two adult males.

"Daddy said we should try to make people feel better."

She nodded. "He was right."

Nolan offered her a card. "You need anything, you call me, Jasmine."

Behind her Lance muttered, "She won't."

Jasmine smiled and took the card. "Thank you. It was a great pleasure sharing ice cream with you today, Liam."

"Bye, Jasmine. Nice to meet you."

A brisk nod to the father and she walked away, Lance draping his arm around her shoulders and brushing a kiss along her cheek.

"We really need to talk about this, baby."

Chapter Fourteen

*Yesterday is not ours to recover,
but tomorrow is ours to win or lose.
~ Lyndon B. Johnson*

The anger he'd been holding at bay raged within him. A mix of crap from Robert and from seeing his woman with some handsome man who was absolutely, hands-down flirting with her. As they walked he tried to calm himself, but it wasn't working. All he could see in his mind was Jasmine and that man in an erotic setting. The man's hands skimming down her curves. Peeling her clothing off her one article at a time, exposing the smooth brown skin.

A growl erupted from his chest and he damn near dragged her deep into the nearest alley. She didn't fight him, however when he had her pinned between himself and the wall, he noticed the confusion in her expression.

"You." The single word fell from his lips, nearly feral.

Part of him expected a glib comment, for that was Jasmine, always with the quick retorts. Not this time. She held still, almost as if she knew sudden movements would spur the predator within him to hunting mode.

"Are you fucking kidding me right now, Jasmine?"

She dragged her tongue along her lower lip and he pounced with a snarl. The hand that had been clamped around her wrist as he dragged her behind him moved up and manacled along the front of her neck. His thumb kept her chin up so he could devour her.

With a bruising grip on her hip, he ground his hard erection into her as he slipped that hand up to wrap around her ponytail. He growled as he pulled back, nipped her lip and kept them nose to nose.

"You don't get to decide to do something foolish and risky. We're not done. *I'm* not done with you."

He heard the wobble in his voice that appeared at the mere thought of losing her—to another man or to the insanity that surrounded them with the mob and the FBI fuckup.

He kissed her again, needing to have her beneath him. To feel her soften for him, allow him to command her body as he'd spent the past while doing. Hear her admit that it was only him she would lower her guard for. Only him who could elevate her to such heights. Only him, from this moment on, who would ever touch her.

Her tongue met his as he plundered her mouth. Opening beneath him, she allowed him to take what he wanted.

It wasn't enough.

It wouldn't *ever* be enough for him. Not when it came down to one fiery woman named Jasmine Hoyer.

Moving his touch from her hip, he slid his hand between her legs and cupped her core. Nipping at her tongue when she shuddered, he tightened his hold on her throat and chin, not allowing her to move away.

Anger raged within him. A need to dominate. To possess.

It roared over him, like a tsunami racing toward shore. He didn't even try to stop it. In fact, he embraced it.

Tearing his mouth from hers, he held her gaze. Lance had expected her fury to be waiting. That she wouldn't be happy with his manhandling. What he got shocked him. There was no aggression in her gaze or stance. She wasn't trying to push him away or get him to be gentler. Jasmine held his stare, waiting for him to make his next move.

"Mine."

It was the only word he could push through his lips. She settled her hands on either side of his face and yanked his mouth back to hers. Squeezing her thighs around his hand between her legs, she moaned as she stabbed her tongue deep into his mouth.

Yanking his hand from between her legs, he slapped his palm against the wall behind her. "I'm seconds away from fucking you right here."

She wound her arms around his neck and laughed. "If that's supposed to be a threat, you're off base. Way off base."

"I don't want anyone to see what's mine."

Jasmine leaned forward. "Let's go before I have to kill some women for looking at yours."

They took the long way to get back to the safe house, using the bus and making sure that no one was following them by backtracking and the like. The moment they made it back to the apartment, he had her up against the wall, her pants off and his dick so far inside her he could feel her heartbeat.

****

Four hours later, after several rounds of fucking — that's what it had been, nothing else but hard fucking — he woke to find her not in the bed. Frowning, he rolled to his feet and tugged on some dark blue workout pants before padding up the hallway.

Jasmine stood at the window looking out, tiny pale pink shorts barely covering the globes of her ass while her matching cami made his cock stand at attention. The lace at the top allowed him to see a teasing hint of her high and firm breasts. He licked his lips and propped his shoulder against the doorframe.

"Ready to talk?" She didn't glance away from the window when she posed her question.

While he longed to cross over to her and tug her close, he stayed put, acknowledging that he had to keep his distance or his dick would be fully sunk inside her in seconds. He couldn't get enough.

"Explain." Lance frowned over the growl in his tone.

Now she turned toward him. He bit his lower lip as he skimmed her front. How the fuck did this woman ruin him and turn him into a horny teen who basically lived by and for his dick?

A shoulder bounce. "Nothing to explain. You did what you had to, as did I."

He gritted his teeth. "Disagree. You deliberately put yourself in danger. Then, as I had to track you down, when I locate you, I find you getting all cozy with some hot-ass man and his kid, looking like a family."

"So I should have smacked a kid who was being nice to me because he saw me crying?" She strode over the floor to him and propped her hands on shapely hips.

Lance gulped hard, reached out and snagged the waistband of those going-to-be-the-death-of-him shorts, pulling her flush to his bare chest. The urge to go scorched earth slammed him. "Why were you crying?" His tone was low and about five hundred nautical miles beyond feral.

She flattened her lips and shook her head in the familiar brisk Jasmine "Nothing Gets to Me" Hoyer way.

"Fuck no," he muttered, gripping her throat as he'd done in the alley. His thumb moved slowly along her lower lip, caressing, even as his hold was absolute. "Talk to me, baby. Why were you crying? Who do I need to kill? I'm happy to start with that dick who bought my woman ice cream."

She cocked an eyebrow at his statement but he didn't refute it. Fuck no, he meant every word. Every. Single. One.

"It's stupid." She shook her head, or rather tried to, but he refused to allow it.

"Never diminish your feelings, baby. It's not stupid." He softened his touch and tugged her closer, spreading his left hand over her ass cheek, fingertips caressing the soft skin below the hem of her shorts. "Tell me."

She closed her eyes and took a deep, shuddering breath. "I'd called Caro."

God damn it he wanted to make all her pain go away. "How is she? Your nephew? Declan?" He'd gotten along fairly well with Declan McBride when they'd been protecting Caro, who had—unbeknownst to the law—taken Jasmine's place, but since he'd gone under, he hadn't reached out and made contact. At all.

Had there been a man he would have considered a friend, it was Declan.

Tears glistened in her gorgeous big brown eyes. They didn't fall. "I didn't say a word but it's like she knew it was me. Said she missed me, they missed me and they loved me."

Her voice cracked on that last admission and her legs wobbled. Turning them so the wall supported her back and wedging a leg between her legs, he kept her there. Her heated core was on his thigh and he groaned low in his throat when she rocked on him. Clenching his jaw, he didn't respond. This was an avoidance tactic he knew well. Distract him with sex.

Normally he was all-in for that, but right now his woman needed more than just physical from him. Tightening his grip on her neck, he waited for her gaze to slide back to his.

"Talk to me, baby."

Her plump lower lip trembled. He leaned close and dragged his nose along her face, inhaling her subtle and all-too-fucking addictive scent.

"I miss her, okay?" The four words were sharp and angry. Accusatory almost. "She's my fucking twin and I miss her." Jasmine's voice broke on the admission and Lance's heart did the same.

* * * *

She ached. *And not in that good, I've been fucked within an inch of my life ache. More like the I bawled like a baby ache.*

Jasmine Hoyer rolled over in the queen-sized bed, flopping her face into the pillow that smelled like

Lance. He'd done it. Gotten her walls to not simply drop but fucking shatter.

Raw. Exposed. Vulnerable.

Nothing she'd allowed herself to be since she'd escaped the second abusive foster home. But this man, this arrogant, sexy-as-sin detective who was risking his life going undercover, had revealed it all.

"Gahhh!" She screamed in the pillow before punching it then leveraging up and off the bed. He'd rolled from bed maybe ten minutes before her.

Naked, she made her way to the bathroom and allowed herself a swift shower. Normally, lingering would be something to indulge in but this morning her emotions were still too open and she would think about how Lance was getting to her far more than she wanted to let him, or had believed she would ever allow someone to. Dwell. Sink further into her head.

Barely pausing to dry off, she pulled her light gray cut-off sweats up over her ice blue thong before tugging on her pale green razorback tee. She tossed her hair up in a messy bun as she walked up the hallway.

Lance stood in the kitchen over the stovetop frying some eggs and bacon. Shirtless.

Honestly it wasn't fair. No man should be like this when they first woke up. Not that he changed the longer the day went on, but still. Not fair. Without looking away from the food he worked on, he reached out his right arm and, without hesitation, she walked right into him, allowing him to drape that arm around her shoulder and tuck her close.

"Morning."

She tucked her thumb in the waistband of his unbuttoned jeans. For a moment they merely stood there, the act domestic in its simplicity. She allowed herself a moment of fantasy where this was her every day. Her. Him.

All she needed.

He leaned closer and brushed a kiss over her temple. "I'll bring you some food, take a seat."

Jasmine was halfway to the table before it registered she'd not even hesitated to follow his command. A low chuckle followed her as if he'd read her very thought on the matter. Within five minutes there was a hearty breakfast before each of them, complete with orange juice and coffee.

Instead of sitting across the small table from her, he'd moved the chair he occupied to right beside her, ensuring their legs touched. But he didn't stop there, no, of course not. This man buttered and put jam on her toast, he cut up her potatoes for her, and she didn't doubt he would have fed her if she'd not put a stop to that.

"I'm capable." Her words were gruff.

"I am very aware of how capable you are, Jasmine. Doesn't mean I stop wanting to take care of you. Providing for you. *Protecting* you."

Swallowing down her immediate response, she picked up the toast piece he'd slathered with butter and loganberry jam. A favorite of hers since she'd moved out here, it was a hybrid of blackberry and raspberry. Indulging in a large bite, she watched him in her periphery as she chewed. Slowly.

He observed her in return and once she swallowed, he picked up the toast she'd just taken a bite of and held it back out to her, offering a second. They ate slowly, more often than not him feeding her. But he didn't try to force her into conversation.

A good thing because she was still raw from yesterday. That much confessing wasn't easy. Her walls were thick and it had been harsh seeing the world without their protection.

Lance took the dishes away when they finished and together they cleaned up. As she wrapped up wiping off the final counter, someone knocked on the door. Weapons in hand, seconds later they moved in tandem to the door. When they were in proper position, she opened the door and scowled.

"What the fuck are you doing here?"

Lance moved closer and grunted. "How did you find us?"

Robert stood there, blood dripping down his head and covered in dirt and lord knew what else. The man wobbled and gripped the doorframe in one hand.

"I need your help."

His voice was a wheeze. Jasmine narrowed her gaze but didn't say a word. She didn't trust this bastard as far as she could toss him. And given what had happened to Lance, she didn't think he would either but the man hadn't shot him yet, so what did she know? Then there was the fact he didn't answer how he'd found them.

Lance glanced at her before moving her back slightly to open the door a bit more so Robert could enter.

Well, she knew the sliver of betrayal that dripped down her spine and wound around her heart wasn't one she would be able to ignore. Every single instinct she possessed screamed at her to curl her index finger around the trigger and pull, ending the betrayer's life.

Had she the anger she used to carry she probably would have, but hating people who'd wronged her took up too much of her energy and she had other things to do. Right now, that included figuring out why the man she'd fallen for was siding with the one who had nearly gotten her, and him, killed.

The minute the door clicked shut, Lance handed over his sidearm to her and immediately frisked the bleeding man before them.

"He's clean."

She doubted it but didn't say a word, merely handed the weapon back to Lance and stepped away.

"Let's get him fixed up." Lance guided Robert to the kitchen table.

His phrasing didn't go unnoticed by Jasmine and she sneered at their backs. Instead of following the men to the kitchen, she went to the bedroom and changed out of her sleep clothes.

Lance entered the room as she tugged her cargo pants up over her ass. He stared at her as she fastened them then tucked the SIG in the waistband. No words were spoken as she grabbed a charcoal gray ribbed tee and drew it over her head.

"Jasmine," he said, licking his lips and coming closer. "I know you don't want to see him, but he needs our help."

Her heart was breaking. It was official. After yesterday and now this, she didn't have a lot to give. Normally she'd wear something different out of the apartment but she didn't care right now. And she longed for clothing that made her feel comfortable. Anything to help combat the iciness coating her insides.

"Do what you need to."

It was like swallowing razorblades getting those words out. He stared at her, unblinking until he moved close and slipped his hand around the nape of her neck and pressed a slow, lingering kiss to her lips. She couldn't help it, sinking into him was natural and perfect.

"Thank you for understanding," he murmured as he drew back. "I'll see you out there." He grabbed his shirt on the way out of the room.

Swiftly braiding her hair, she tied it off and swiped her go-bag from the closet. This place was burned. She wouldn't ever feel comfortable resting her head at a place that Robert knew existed.

Years of being on her own while hiding from the company that had betrayed her wasn't about to be wiped away because the man she was fucking wanted to trust him. Dropping to her knee, she cast one look to the door before reaching under the simple end table and depressing the panel there. It slid away and she dipped her hand in and pulled out the mini folio then shoved it into her bag. Another peek to the door and she replaced the panel.

Bringing her bag with her on the way out of the room, she ducked into the bathroom. She knew her shit and had an exit in there. As she shimmied out the window and jumped to the fire escape, she cast one last look over her shoulder as if she could peer through the walls and actually lay eyes on Lance.

"Goodbye, Lance." Her words fell barely above a whisper.

Slipping away into the people on the sidewalk, she ignored the tears that threatened and didn't look back.

Chapter Fifteen

Let your plans be dark and impenetrable as night, and when you move, fall like a thunderbolt.
~ Sun Tzu

"I'm going to kill you myself if this ends up being a trap." Lance didn't even look over to the man who was beside him at the window of an empty apartment building as they overlooked the building across the street.

"How many times do I have to tell you, I didn't betray you. I didn't betray your woman either."

Lance scowled and pulled his gaze from the scene before him to glare over to the man with him. "Fuck you."

"Don't blame me. She decided to leave. I didn't make her do that."

"Not this time anyway."

Robert snorted, eyes never wavering from the window. "I had my own orders."

"Whatever." Readjusting, Lance took up his position once more and watched the faded red brick building. It was showing signs of age, a few bricks missing sporadically around the front and the side he could see. The windows were a mixture of covered by different threadbare curtains and shades to having none or being open.

He assumed the rooms there were like they were here — small with low and water-stained ceilings. Dirty, smudged and grimy windows. A few windows across the way had precariously balanced air conditioning units with jerry-rigged support.

Lance knew the lights above him would flicker when it got dark, a fact they'd noticed happening when they first arrived.

"Look. I know you don't want to be with me. Don't trust me like you should and I get it. There's a lot that happened which shouldn't have. But you were smart and didn't trust that woman you were fucking—"

"Shut your fucking mouth, Robert" — his entire body tensed — "or I'll fucking shut it for you."

"You have to know she left for a reason. She could have stayed and helped us. Okay, you. But she didn't. She ran. Fuck, for all I know she was in on the—"

Lance slammed him up against the wall, not in the window even though it was closer. Hand closing around his windpipe, Robert sputtered and tried to fight Lance off but he couldn't get a foothold. Too many years of watching from a desk had weakened him, softened him. And his most recent injuries didn't help.

On the other hand, Lance had a level of rage he'd never experienced before on his side. Nostrils flaring, he pushed his face right in that of Robert, aware his expression was a feral snarl. The man stammered and spittle formed at the corners of his mouth. Lance squeezed harder.

"That woman isn't here because I betrayed her by choosing to go against my gut and her to help you. She is the victim, don't fucking try to pretend you are. I know about orders, I lived them too. Military. Law enforcement. But what we didn't do in the military that I see all you FBI dicks, CIA asshats, whatever group, are happy to do, is leave a man behind. Let one take the blame. Sacrifice one to save the many, and that's not fucking okay with me." Tighter yet. "Especially when it's *my* woman you did it to."

He couldn't rid himself of the pounding in his ears, his adrenaline rush or the pulse that had kicked up more than a few notches. With a snarl, Lance stepped back from Robert, not giving a damn when he sank to the floor in a heap, gasping and rubbing at his neck as he was allowed air once more. Red tinged his vision. He needed this to wrap the fuck up so he could hunt Jasmine down.

Struggling to calm his emotions, he paced back and forth, knowing he had to focus on this task so he could turn his attention to the far more important one— Jasmine.

"Fuck you," Robert snarled. "I thought you were going to kill me."

"I was." A simple shrug. "But it would take time because I would have to wipe this place down." He reclaimed his position by the window and watched. According to his timepiece the meet should be starting in three minutes.

"Christ, it sounds like you've fucking fallen in love."

"Not your goddamn business." He didn't look away from the building entrance.

"You know she was a whore and a drug addict." Derision filled Robert's tone.

"I know she did what she did in order to survive. She isn't a whore and she doesn't do drugs now. In fact, she has risen back to her rightful place at the top despite all the shit your people threw at her." Angling his head slightly to see the man stumbling to his spot by the other window, he sneered in his direction. "I understand why she didn't trust you or your people. Just like I understand why her name makes your ass pucker. Because she is the best you had, you lost her, and knowing she is back and could blow up whatever op went sideways in your faces, well, it scares the shit out of you. And it should."

A black SUV pulled up and he clamped his jaw shut. Tension rose in the room as he watched four men pour out. Federal agents. *Never did know how to blend in.* They spoke into their wrist pieces and spread out as the vehicle moved on. One of them stopped before entering the building and glanced around, lasering in on the building they were in.

Lance froze, and in his periphery he noticed Robert doing the same thing. Unease skittered up his spine and he narrowed his gaze.

What are the chances this is nothing but another setup?

He feared those chances were astronomically high. A low rumble rolled up from his chest. *Was I a fucking idiot and trusted this man only to find myself in the situation my Jasmine had been in?*

Another vehicle paused in front of the building and three others got out. There was no missing the way they tugged shirts over weapons. As subtly as he could, he shifted his body to take in Robert as well.

I fucked up, royally.

By the snort coming from Robert, the move wasn't something that he didn't miss. Lance didn't give a fuck. Right now he had a singular focus, get out of here alive so he could track down his woman.

And grovel for her forgiveness.

"Fuck." Robert lurched away from the window.

Lance glanced out and threw himself back just as a plethora of bullets shattered the glass. Rolling, he popped back up to his feet, palming his sidearm. As he bit back a curse, or twelve, he looked out again, seeing Dusan Jankovic and his men rushing across the street toward the building he was currently in.

"Help me."

Lance gazed to Robert and shook his head. The man had a bullet wound in his gut and had sunk to his knees, hand clasped over the hole.

"How the fuck did they know we were here?" Not that he needed an answer, he had it.

"I had to give him something. My family…"

"If you weren't already dying because of that wound, I'd fucking kill you myself. If there is any chance you make it out of here and I see you again, you'll wish you'd let Jasmine kill you for the hell I will put you through."

There was so much more he longed to say to this man, but he knew his time for getting out alive was dwindling. Still…

He punched him in the jaw, taking precious seconds to enjoy his head snapping back before running for the door. Instead of going down, he took a deep breath and headed up. There was no point in calling the cops, not unless he wanted to have deaths on his conscience.

Dashing up three flights, he headed for the roof and kicked open the door. Checking his position, he ran for the far side and pulled up short.

Fuck me.

He had to jump. Stepping away from the edge, he tucked his sidearm in the back of his jeans and rubbed his chest, which still fucking hurt from the beatdown he'd taken from Dusan's idiot son. It was going to hurt.

One last deep breath and he ran for the edge, launching himself off at the last possible second. Arms flailing as he bridged the gap, he grunted in pain as he landed and rolled.

Weapon in hand again, he ran for the access door. It was locked. Finding a pipe not far away, he wrenched the piece from its housing and smashed off the outside doorknob. When the chassis and spindle fell, he spun the pipe then punched through the borehole, sending rest of the components through to fall inside. Without the rest of the structure holding it secure, the latch assembly was barely any resistance for him to get inside.

Sweat dripped down his body as he finally made it back to the first floor. Yep, he could use a few more weeks of recovery before doing shit like this again. He glanced out the door before slipping out and heading up the street away from the shitshow to cross the street and go down behind the apartments and up the alley. Thankfully it was full of dumpsters that he could dip behind as he moved to the end he needed to be at.

Peering around the corner, he sucked in a breath. "Fucking hell."

The street was basically empty, as he figured happened in the Old West when gunslingers were facing off. Two dark SUVs were at angles, blocking the street and leaving an opening between the building he was in the alley of and the one he'd been hiding in.

But that wasn't what pulled the curse from his lips. Dusan stood in the middle of the street, a bleeding Robert on his left and Mark on his right with Dusan's muscle making a half circle around him. Ensuring Lance wasn't getting away.

Not that he looked like he was up to go anywhere fast. No, Lance figured when Jasmine had brought him to the safehouse after his ass had been kicked, he looked similar.

"Come out, Lance Beckner, and I will spare their lives."

Right. *Sure* he would.

Michal strolled into view, his black shirt opened, showing off his pathetic chest. "I don't see him." He pulled his gun and aimed it at Robert. "You said he was here with you."

The Fed sneered. "He is. It's not my fault you couldn't find him. From what I understand you can't find your asshole and have to have your bodyguards do it for you."

Digging for his phone, Lance stepped back into the shadows and dialed a number that had been listed as Booty Call in his phone. *I should have done this sooner.* He sent a text and took a deep breath before following that up with a call and shoving the phone in his back pocket. Then he stepped into view.

Jasmine ignored the blood sliding over the back of her hand as she lay upon the roof. The angle wasn't perfect, but she did have a bead on the scum-sucking Dusan Jakovich.

She was well on her way—broken heart and all—to increasing the distance between her and Lance Beckner, or Baldwin. He'd made his decision and as much as she wanted to hate him for it, she couldn't. Did she trust him now? After all, he'd made his stance clear and again, maybe if she weren't dealing with her own broken heart, she would be angry.

I should have known. I don't get a happily ever after.

It was called paying her dues. She'd been a shit person for many years and she had penance to deal with. However, her California exit had been waylaid as she'd gotten to Mark's apartment to say her farewells in time to see him getting dragged away by Dusan's men and shoved into the back of a black SUV.

Sorrow had instantly shoved to the back of her thoughts as anger and the need for vengeance rose swiftly. The man had tried to have her killed, she gotten over it. He wasn't the first. He'd tried to have Lance killed. Upsetting? Yes, but the man was an undercover cop. It wasn't the first time for him either.

But her friend? Single father? Hell to the fuck no.

Scorched earth was a saying. And that bastard was going to get to see it up close and personal. She'd followed, her unease growing as she'd realized where their destination was going to be. Hopping out a block away, she'd tossed cash at the driver and began to jog.

It hadn't taken too much for her to make her way up to the roof of the building she entered then to jump across to get to the one she needed to be at, her bag slamming into her back and shoulder with each jump.

Positioned as she was where the shadow wouldn't give away her location, she peeked over the edge of the roof, making sure Dusan was still in her line of sight. Gaze zeroing in on Mark and his beaten body as he somehow stood there.

"Damn it, Mark, why didn't you just tell them what they wanted to know?" Her words were laced with tears she refused to allow free. He never failed to try to protect her.

This was all her fault. Because she'd brought him in when she needed help with Lance. And that man had repaid her loyalty by siding with the Fed who had betrayed them all.

Her phone buzzed against her hip and she lowered herself from view and dug it out to stare at the number. No one should have this number other than Lance and Mark.

She didn't recognize it. But the area code did ring familiar in her mind. Wisconsin.

"Hello?" Jasmine lifted herself up a tiny bit and peered over again.

"Jasmine? It's Declan McBride."

She fell back. *Fuck my life. What else can go wrong?* And it had to be wrong for a man who reviled her to call. "Is Caro okay? DJ?" She didn't have the energy to tighten her core and peer over the edge while having this conversation, whatever it was supposed to be.

She and Declan hadn't ever gotten along. She'd made his life hell and he'd never attempted to make her think he liked her in the slightest. But all that had changed when he'd married her twin. Jasmine did her best not to antagonize him. She'd just gotten her sister back and didn't want to put her in the position where she had to choose.

"I'm supposed to tell you not to do anything foolish." A grunt. "Now that that's out of the way, I heard from our mutual friend and have been updated on the situation. I've made some calls and there are people on the way both to your current location and to the Jankovic house for his attempt on law enforcement's life."

"Why are you calling me?" Leveraging up on her elbow, she peered over the edge once more, frowning as Dusan's son strolled into view.

"Believe me, not anything I care to do but—"

She hung up on him, needing to focus on the scene before her. Her twin was fine, her nephew was fine, and honestly that's all she cared about.

Shit. I have to get down there. The father was bad enough, but when his son, his highly unstable son, showed up, this is when things went sideways. Crouched, she skimmed the edge, searching for the fire escape. The second she fired her first shot, they would have her location and she would have to get moving.

Another peek over the side and she palmed her sidearm. She didn't have any way of hearing the conversation happening street level, but she would have to be blind to miss the escalating anger between the parties.

A low rumble rolled from her chest as Michel backhanded Mark, rocking his head on his shoulders. The man stumbled but held himself upright once more. Lifting his chin, he spat out a response.

She knew him well. He'd made his peace with whatever was going to happen to him. And she also knew him well enough to know he would sacrifice himself for her. Settling against the corner, she set her aim.

I've never wished more for a sniper rifle.

Her phone buzzed against her ass cheek but she didn't move. She wasn't aiming at Dusan, no, her bead was on Michel. The hot-headed young upstart who thought he couldn't do any wrong. Thought his shit didn't stink and he could get away with anything because of who his daddy was.

The firehose. Fuck, yes! Staying low, she crouch-waddled to the thick roll of firehose. *Here's hoping you're fucking fifty meters and not thirty-six.* SIG by her knee, she unrolled the heavy hose enough to loop it around her waist and give it the best knot she could finagle.

As she unlocked the roll so it would spin unincumbered, she went back to the edge and peered over. *What the fuck is he doing there?*

Lance walked into view, drawing the attention of both Dusan and Michel. Robert was bleeding, looked like from his gut and head. She recognized the head injury but the gut one…that was new.

Not a shred of sympathy for him. Bastard could bleed out for all she cared. Checking her magazine, she took a deep breath and sighted again. Lance was shaking his head and gesturing at Mark. Michel puffed out his unimpressive chest and stepped in front of Lance.

She snorted a laugh as Lance barely hesitated, just threw a punch, knocking him to the ground.

Good job.

Dusan's men drew on him when he stepped toward their boss. All she could see was a lot of gesturing and Michel struggling to get back on his feet. No one helped him and when he finally managed to accomplish that, he drew his gun and aimed it at Lance. At the last second, he adjusted slightly and shot by Lance's head and killed Mark.

She'd retaliated before her friend's body even hit the ground. With a yell, she fired at Michel as she leaped over the edge and began running, just like she'd learned to do years ago when she'd learned Australian abseiling during one of her many courses. Yes, she was a sitting duck but it didn't matter. They would pay.

She'd taken out two of their men before they'd realized what she was doing. Lance dove out of the way even as he glanced up at her as he rolled. She watched him mouth her name, then she focused again on Dusan and his men. As well as Michel's men.

Two slugs tore into her left shoulder and side and she nearly dropped her gun before she could switch to her right.

"Jasmine!"

Everything happened at once, and yet, at the same time, it was like in slow motion.

She didn't waste time yelling back, needing Lance to realize he had to focus on keeping himself alive. Dusan's men were doing their best to protect their boss. Lance began firing. In her periphery she noticed Robert went down but her focus was on Mark and holding onto every shred of hope in the universe that her friend was still alive.

Her body jerked as the reel lurched forward. Yeah, this may not have been the smartest idea ever. Her back pocket began buzzing once again, pushing a bit of hysterical laughter from her.

I'm running down the side of a building, praying the fire hose knotted at my waist doesn't give out before the reel it's attached to careens over the edge, like I have time to pause in that and the firefight to answer my phone.

Another lurch forward and she figured they were firing at the hose now, trying to get it to tear and plummet her. Two stories left. Ejecting the empty magazine, she pulled out another and slammed it home and began firing once more.

Her makeshift repel rope jerked her to a hard stop, left her there for a few seconds, then gave away about ten feet above the ground and she fell. Hard.

Immediately rolling, she came up as fast as she could. Her right knee hurt like hell and was nearly non-weight-bearing. Scanning the area for Dusan, she tried to slow her breathing as she cased the view, needing to be calm, be focused. Needed to be ready for anything. Bodies littered the streets and sirens screamed in the distance.

Moving around the side of a haphazardly parked SUV, she found him. Robert's body was a crumpled heap not too far away, but the man she sought had no weapon and two holes in his leg. Lance was over him, weapon trained and looking far more like the detective she'd once propositioned than the bad boy undercover agent to whom she'd lost her heart.

"You know," Lance said, not looking away from Dusan even as he beckoned her closer. "Declan says next time he fucking calls you pick up."

She went to him because she was powerless to do anything but that. He angled himself so he could see both her and Dusan.

"You okay?"

Her eyes went to Mark and she shook her head. "Starting to think I'm getting too old for this shit."

Bastard nodded. Then he gripped her chin and kissed her. "You should find a nice man to settle down with and raise some kids."

"You'll never get away from me. I will hunt you down and kill you. Kill your family, your kids, hell, I may even kill your parents," Dusan raged.

Lance moved to his side and whispered something in his ear. Jasmine walked over to Mark's body and whimpered as she sank to the ground beside him. He was gone.

"I'm so sorry, Mark. You stupid fuck, you had a kid. Why didn't you just give them what they wanted?" Tears streamed as she collapsed onto his chest.

Law enforcement arrived and she was pulled away from Mark by Lance, who held her close as he escorted her to the ambulance so they could check her knee. Two federal marshals walked up and showed badges.

"Ms. Hoyer, Mr. Baldwin?"

They nodded. Lance shifted to partially protect her. All she could think about was Den, Mark's now parentless son, and how she had to get to him.

"We're here to take you in and debrief from the undercover operation."

"Give us a minute." Lance's tone booked no room for argument. Even the EMT gave them space. He captured her face in his hands, thumbs smoothing along her skin.

"Baby," he said softly. "I'm so fucking sorry I didn't choose you. Biggest mistake of my life."

She removed his touch from her face, noting how his expression became pained but she couldn't think of his feelings, not right now. "I have to get to Den. I'm all he has left now."

Lance nodded. Once. Firm. "What do you need from me?"

"A diversion, and you to get my bag from the roof."

"Consider it done. And, baby? When we meet up after this, because we sure as hell will, I'm taking you over my knee for jumping off the fucking roof like that." He kissed her once. Hard. "Go get our son. I'll find you."

He walked off and did what he'd promised. Created a diversion. Went right after Dusan, leaving her to slip away like a shadow. Like her namesake. Smoke.

Epilogue

Eleven months later

Mist rolled off the lake, slow and beautiful. Morning sunrise cast the land in warm, soft, golden light. The cabin sat tucked into the grove of trees, protected yet with a direct line of sight to the dock leading out into the lake. This morning, however, even the dock was shrouded in the otherworldly haze.

Grunts and the sounds of wood colliding echoed through the woods and off the water.

A young boy dashed from the protection of the trees, his dusky skin aglow in the morning light. A mopful of loose dark curls bounced with each of his rapid steps. A wooden sword was gripped in one hand as he pumped his arms, running toward the cabin.

Chest heaving, he whipped around and faced the woods, lower lip resting between his teeth. He shifted his stance, as if he couldn't quite figure out how best to set himself. Dirt-stained fingers flexed around the hilt as he stared, even squinting, as if that could help his vision.

Only the tendrils of fog moved, winding up from the lake to wrap around his ankles as if anchoring him in place. He gulped.

"Auntie?"

Nothing moved from the forest. No birds chirped. No animals chattered.

He stepped forward. "Auntie?"

A branch cracked and he jumped to the right, toward the lake. But nothing happened. No one appeared. It remained still.

A warrior cry rent the air. The boy jerked, eyes wide as he glanced around. Behind him a woman ran toward him, her own sword brandished as she snarled.

He screamed and ran, this time toward the water. The sword fell to the hard-packed sand around the lake as he streaked toward it, his cry reverberating in the air.

Seven steps from the lake.

Five steps.

He looked behind and screamed again.

Three steps.

One.

"Gotcha!"

She swooped him up and tossed him in the air before catching him. Declan Jr, who she had called DJ from the start, was her first nephew. His sister was sleeping inside but they would play later.

"But, Auntie, I was sooo close." DJ had his lower lip stuck out in a childish pout.

Jasmine laughed with maniacal glee as she growled and nibbled along his neck, making his squeals erupt with screeches of joy. Sinking to her knees, she rolled on the sand with him until he wrapped his thin arms around her neck.

"Love you, Auntie."

She curved her arms around him, anchoring him close to her. "Love you too, DJ." And she meant every word.

Motion in her periphery had her lifting her gaze to find her twin, Carolyn, standing there, eyes soft, hands resting upon her swollen belly. A gentle smile turning up her lips.

Jasmine kept one hand on her nephew's back as she called upon her legs to get them up. Her knee ached, from the building incident, as she referred to it as, but she swallowed down the discomfort.

"Did you see me, Mama? I almost had it. I almost beat her."

"I saw, baby." She canted her head to the side. "Can you go help your daddy with breakfast? I know you and Camden have a lot to do today and need all your energy."

Jasmine let him back to the ground and watched as he ran all-out toward the cabin, spinning around to dash back and get his wooden sword before going hard again. She didn't take her eyes off him or the surrounding area until he was safely inside the cabin. Neither her nor Caro told him to slow down with the wood in his hand. Then she swung her gaze to her sister. Her twin.

Caroline McBride, Caro to friends and family, had found her place in the world. And was living her best life. The brilliant STEM woman's hair had a soft red tint to it in the morning sun. She wore a zippered, midnight-blue hoodie with a gold Atlanta PD logo embroidered on the left side, heather-gray leggings, and a pair of hot-pink shoes.

"Something on your mind?"

Caro looked around and didn't speak for a few moments. "I wanted to spend time with my sister. Is that so wrong?"

Knowing her tone had been sharp, Jasmine took a deep breath. "I don't know. I'm not used to being in close proximity to you." This trip had been Declan and Lance's idea. They'd put it all together. She and Declan were learning to co-exist and she and Lance, well, other than the out-of-the-world sex, she wasn't sure.

He'd tracked her down, fucked her until she legit didn't know her name or have the energy to get up from the pile of blankets she'd woken upon. They were both healing and he had swiftly shut down any talk from her of splitting up. And he treated Camden like his own. Not flinching from the scars or when the young male had a breakdown because his dad was dead and he wasn't sure how to handle it. It had been one hell of a fight to get Lance to head back to Atlanta to his superior because he'd not wanted to leave them. He'd returned within seventy-two hours.

She was so fucking confused it wasn't funny. Jasmine had been granted her life back. In a manner of sorts. The FBI still wanted nothing to do with her and would prefer she disappear off the face of the earth, but they had agreed to leave her alone if she kept her information locked up in a vault and never speak of it, ever. She had nodded but refused to sign anything, well aware that once she was gone, they could shred the paper they signed to not have to uphold their end all the while they could, and would, keep her signed form of compliance. So she made sure the director was well aware that there was proof that would come to light if they ever thought about coming after her or her, Lance, or Caro and Declan.

The Jankovic family criminal enterprise had been shut down, their human trafficking ring, gun running, and drug trade put to rest. She wasn't foolish enough to think someone else wouldn't just pop up and start it up again, but that one had been ended. Part of Lance heading back to Atlanta was to get his old job back. Lance Beckner with blue-green eyes had been laid to rest, allowing Atlanta Detective Lance Baldwin with the icy green eyes to return.

The man had been adamant he wasn't leaving her, no matter what she said. Damn it all if the part of her who yearned for what her twin had for her life hadn't been begging for her to believe him and for it to be true.

Personal forgiveness wasn't anything she was good with doing.

Caro stepped closer and settled a hand on her arm. "Are you worried for our safety?"

It took her a great deal not to flinch at the touch. She had no wish to hurt her sister's feelings but personally, she was still learning about this public affection. Or any at all, really, other than from Den and obviously Lance. But with that man, it was the ground she understood. Sex was a language she spoke fluently, her difficulty came when it turned deep and intimate. Lance didn't seem in any rush to push her to get to his level.

"Of course I'm worried. You're my sister and you have two small children and a third on the way." She shook her head. Had she not made that clear? That she would do anything to protect her sister and her family?

"And you're mine. Jasmine, we're twins. And we're safe. No one is going to hurt me, or even the kids. I have you, Declan, and Lance."

The three of us may not be enough. She puffed a breath and nodded even as movement at the porch snagged her focus. Lance. He had on an FBI hoodie unzipped halfway, showing off a green shirt and a loose-fitting pair of black sweats. Those damnable green eyes—he no longer wore his contacts—were on her with laser focus. Her breath came short and sharp as a different kind of awareness filled her.

Caro chuckled. "I don't think I'm needed for this. I'll go inside and leave you two to...umm...*explore* before breakfast. I'll tell Declan not to expect you both until later, and when Den gets up, we'll let him know you're out on a walk. The way he's looking at you is how Declan looked at me before this happened." Laughter tinged her sentences as she gestured to her swollen belly. "Again."

Before Jasmine could say a word, Caro kissed her on the cheek and walked away. She squeezed Lance's arm briefly as she bypassed him upon entering the cabin. Lance didn't move until the door closed behind her sister. Then he flowed down the steps toward her. Eyes locked on her as he neared, he slipped his hand along the nape of her neck and tugged her so their foreheads touched.

"Morning, baby."

She smelled the coffee on his breath and smiled despite the unease rolling around her gut. Lance Baldwin in her mind was a god among men.

He settled a hand along her cheek. "I missed you this morning." Lance dragged his knuckles down her skin and she could feel her body responding instantly.

"I had a date."

He grunted and kissed her until she sagged into him, boneless and relying on him to keep her upright.

"Don't make me hate on a kid, baby."

"I can't make you do anything." She wrapped her arms around him, happy to simply be with him. The negative woman in her who figured this, whatever it was between them, had an expiration date and she wanted to soak it all up while she could. "Want to take a walk?"

His response was to lead her off toward the forest once more. This time, however, she wasn't holding a wooden sword, nor hunting her nephew. Head resting against his shoulder, she went easily where he led.

"There's something I need to talk to you about, Jasmine." His words were serious and more of that alarm skittered up her back.

She drew away from him and glanced over to his face. He clucked his tongue and pulled her back to him.

"No, no, baby. No pulling away." He guided her along, occasionally brushing a hand along her cheek, tucking some wayward hair behind her ear. Never letting her even consider he wasn't paying attention to her.

They came upon an area with a few larger, overturned trunks. Cool morning wind blew through the towering trees that rose from the earth and strained to brush the sky. Shadows flickered, created from some sun-dappled leaves. The moss that wound around trunks and rocks had leaves and pine needles captured within. There were plenty of pinecones dotting the ground, as if a toy chest of precious trinkets had been tipped.

Lance encouraged her to sit on one of the trunks. She didn't like this.

He gave a rough chuckle. "Baby, you look like you're about to hurl in my direction." Moving between her legs, he settled his hands along the sides of her face.

The idea was possible. Highly probable. She shifted on the rough wood. "I'm not sure what you're looking for from me."

His tongue dipped out to skim over his lower lip and her belly clenched in response. "What I want? After everything we've been through, you're not sure what I want from you?" His voice had risen in volume and was drenched in disbelief mixed with anger.

She narrowed her gaze, not at all appreciating him getting huffy with her, she'd been honest. "No need to yell at me, I was just asking a fucking—"

He slammed his mouth over hers, taking no prisoners, thrusting his tongue deep and growling when she followed his lead. A rumble rolled up from his chest when he broke the kiss.

Heads touching, he dragged his thumb over her lower lip. "Everything."

Jasmine furrowed her brow as he drew back, putting a tiny bit of space between them.

"I want *everything* from you, baby. You already have me, I want the same. Don't talk to me about how it shouldn't be. *We* work. No matter what excuse you have ready, I'll counter it. I want you with me, morning, noon, and night. I was thinking about what Mark said. Private investigators. We can take cases we want, go where we want. But we'll be together. I can't without you, Jasmine. I *can't* do it. Not without you and Camden."

Heart thundering nearly out of control, Jasmine watched him. Saw beneath the assured, nearly cocky look to uncertainty, and a hint of desperation. Of a need so powerful, this man was willing to bare his vulnerability to her.

There were hundreds of excuses she could provide why it was wrong. Why they were wrong for each other. And she didn't doubt he would have hundreds of counters to hers.

Gripping his sweatshirt, she yanked him right back to her lips. "Yes."

"Fucking finally," he groaned against her mouth as he took possession of it once more.

They didn't leave the forest for another hour, and as they walked back to the cabin, she was sated and content, her hand rested his. They didn't rush, merely enjoying being with each other. Jasmine didn't know what their future would hold but with Lance and Den along with Caro and her family, she had no doubt it would be full and overflowing with love.

Maybe I can learn to let others in. And let myself learn how to be loved without expecting something to be paid back.

They walked into the cabin and found everyone's attention locked on them. Den and DJ were seated together. Caro and Declan's daughter, Mary—who went by Mae and who'd been named for the first African American woman to earn a PhD in chemistry in the US but also in honor of the numerous other Marys who were trailblazers in their fields—was curled up in her father's lap, adorably sleepy in her science-themed pajamas.

The boys paused in eating and skimmed over them before shoveling more food in their mouths. "You've got pine needles in your hair, Auntie." DJ shrugged as he made his announcement.

Caro and Declan smirked. The ex-cop rubbed a large hand over his daughter's back. "Bet this entire cabin and the property it has with it that ain't the only place she has them," he teased.

She flushed because he wasn't wrong, there were some in a most uncomfortable place she would be removing when she got to the bedroom. Lance outright laughed and kissed her temple.

"She's not the only one." He moved by the boys and fist bumped with each of them, Declan included, brushed a kiss along Caro's cheek and moved into the kitchen. "Come get some food, baby. I know you're hungry."

Caro waggled her eyebrows, and this time she found herself smiling without wondering if it was going to cost her later. She made it three steps before her phone rang. Her ease faded in less than a second as she pulled out her phone. The only people who had her number were here in the cabin with her.

Lance watched her from the kitchen and placed the plates in his hands on the counter. "Everything okay, baby?"

She blinked at the name on the screen. "I don't know. It's Nolan."

A low growl left Lance and he moved toward her as she hovered over the accept button. Like she was in a tunnel, she heard Lance fill them in on who Nolan was as she tapped the button.

"Nolan?" she said by way of answering.

"I need your help, Jasmine." The line went dead.

"Nolan?" Jasmine asked even though she couldn't hear him. Uncertainty rushed in fast, digging its claws in deep. Lifting her gaze, she found Lance right there beside her, his hand pressing on the small of her back.

"Baby?"

She shook her head. "I don't know. He said he needed my help then the line went dead." She tried to call the phone back but all she got was a message that the number couldn't be completed as dialed. "He has a son, Lance."

"I know baby. We'll get to him and help in any way we can." He kissed her cheek. "Then we're going to talk about why you have a handsome man's number in your phone and how he got your number."

She barked out a laugh, which from the upturn of his lips had been his intention. Then she sobered. "I didn't." He cocked an eyebrow and she elaborated. "I didn't give him my number. He gave me his card but I hadn't given mine to him."

"We've got Den," Declan said, joining them, reaching out with his hand to squeeze her shoulder. "Go get your man."

Lance snapped his gaze to Declan. "I'm her man, asshole."

Declan rolled his eyes. "And the jealous possessiveness has begun. Fine, go get *Nolan* and help him. We'll keep Den with us and finish up our vacation. Let me know if you need anything."

Jasmine swallowed once and bit the inside of her lower lip before shifting to be directly in front of Declan. He watched her, silent, his hands keeping his young daughter safe and secure.

"Thank you." She blinked. "For everything."

Declan grunted. "We're family." His tone sounded like he'd been gargling glass, but she'd take it because despite the grumping, his gaze sparkled with trouble. She'd take it.

She flicked her focus to Lance.

He nodded. "Got your back, baby. Today, tomorrow, *always*. Let's get going."

Mind centering on the upcoming travel, she calmed. This she understood and could handle. Or so she thought. Lance kissed her until her mind blanked and all she could do was hold him tight as he kissed her dumb.

"We're talking about our wedding on the way." It wasn't a question from him as his hand squeezed her ass. Another quirk of his lips. "I love that freshly fucked and hazy look in your eyes, baby. Let's go save your guy." Another kiss.

"Thank you, Lance."

"Anything for you, baby. You know that."

Yeah, she was figuring that out.

Sign up for our newsletter and find out about all our romance book releases, eBook sales and promotions, sneak peeks and FREE romance books!

Want to see more from this author? Here's a taster for you to enjoy!

Preconception
Aliyah Burke

Excerpt

"I need your help, Carolyn!"

Carolyn Trufant nearly dropped the crystal vase she was filling in the sink. "What's wrong, Jasmine?"

Cars honked. People yelled. The sounds of a busy metropolis's downtown reverberated through the phone line. *Where is she?*

"Help me, please!"

She set the vase down, struggling to hear and decipher the rest of what Jasmine was saying. "I can't hear you."

"…meet me, please."

"Jasmine?" Her voice rose a few notches. "Where do you want me to meet you?"

"Come down to Atlanta, *please*. Meet me where I told you I first visited when I got here. At ten p.m. please, tomorrow. I'm…really scared." The call went dead.

Shit. Carolyn's hands shook like leaves in a stiff breeze. She hung her head and tried to control her racing, out of control emotions.

What could she do? What *should* she do would be a better question.

I have to help her. There's no way I am going to lose her after just finding her.

Caro stroked a finger along the silken petals of the flowers she'd received moments before her sister had called. She loved the variety in the mixture of flowers. *Of course I have to go.*

Allowing herself one more inhalation of the fragrant floral blooms, she swept her gaze around the room, ensuring all items resided in their proper place. Then she went to her office and booked herself a flight to Atlanta.

That evening, once supper had been eaten and cleaned up after, she curled up on one end of her sofa, tucked her feet beneath her and stared through the window of her Madison, Wisconsin, apartment.

She closed her eyes and her thoughts drifted to Jasmine. Her sister. More than that. Her twin. A woman she'd met a month and a half ago. Separated at birth and adopted by other families who didn't know about each other. In fact, even the paperwork stated she had no other known siblings.

To say it had been a shock when Jasmine had first contacted her would be the understatement of the year. Caro had been suspicious, hard not to be when she'd received such a call. She'd asked her parents before about siblings and they'd given her the paperwork, which had denied such things. Still, regardless of her doubts, she'd gone and met her in Saint Louis.

There had been no denying it the moment she'd laid eyes on Jasmine. They'd spent the weekend catching up and learning about one another. Since then they'd exchanged some calls and had discussed having another 'sister' weekend soon. But never a call for help.

She walked to the large window and stared over the twinkling lights of her city. "Never a call with someone sounding so scared either." Caro rested her head against the glass and sighed.

Concerned, she made her way and packed her carry-on. She didn't expect to stay all that long but could take a bit of time off if needed since she had plenty of accumulated days. Lifting the receiver to her landline, she sat on the edge of her bed. She sucked on her lip as she dialed a memorized number. Yes, it was programmed but she did it this way to give herself a bit more time. Not much, true, but anything would be accepted.

"Hello?"

The gentle voice on the other end had her smiling. "Hi, Mama."

"Caro. How are you doing, baby?"

"Fine, Mama. I just wanted to let you and Daddy know I'm taking a short trip." She cleared her throat. "Out of town."

"Hmm. Where to?"

"Down south." She winced, hating the lie she was about to tell. "I have a two week vacation I'm spending in a timeshare."

"Really? You didn't say anything earlier."

Because I didn't know the twin — my twin sister you know nothing about — was going to call me asking for help. "Came up out of the blue. You remember my roommate, Jen? She was going to go but couldn't." She scrunched her eyes and pinched the bridge of her nose. "Just got off the phone with her. I have the time so I figured... Why not?"

More noncommittal noises. "Where down south?"

"Atlanta. I don't have the info yet since she hasn't texted it to me."

"You're leaving when?"

She could see her mother standing there with her head cocked to the side. "Early tomorrow." Late tonight technically but what was one more lie in the grand scheme of things? She was already going to hell.

Her mom, silent for a moment, then made a delicate throat clearing sound. "Have fun and be safe."

"Thanks, Mama." The flush of deceit spread across her neck and face. She despised lying to her parents. "Tell Daddy I say hi. Love to both."

Caro hung up and whimpered.

I feel terrible about this.

Her parents were an amazing couple who'd adopted her and raised her alongside the youngest of their naturally born children. A well-respected couple, they had raised her to understand hard work. When she'd come to Madison for college she hadn't left, and now she worked for the same institution that had supplied her degree. Her boss had been on her case constantly about taking some time off, so she placed a call and left a message on his phone.

Her final call was to her friend who also rented in the same building, Terri Mosse.

"Hello?"

"Hey, Terri. I need a favor."

"Sure thing, babe. What can I do for you?" The blaring music softened. "Everything okay?"

"I'm heading to Atlanta tonight for no more than a couple of weeks."

She whistled low. "Jasmine?"

"Yes." Why did she feel horrible that Terri knew but not her parents?

"You are stressed. What happened?"

"I don't know. She's frightened out of her mind. Asked me to help her." She rubbed the back of her neck. "I can't ignore her. She's my twin."

"I'm not judging, babe. You need to go, go. I will take care of your place. When should I expect you back?"

She pursed her lips. "Not sure. I'm giving myself two weeks if she needs help getting back on her feet. No more than that I wouldn't imagine."

"Your plans change, you let me know."

"I will."

"Caro?"

"Yes, Terri?" She carried her bag to the door.

"Be careful, yeah?"

"I will." They hung up and she pocketed her phone.

She left her apartment, alarm set and door locked, before making her way to the front where she waved for a taxi.

Guilt nagged her as she settled against the leather seat. Her parents—adoptive some may call them, she called them her parents—deserved better than this. They loved her as much as their other children. She'd never felt like she didn't belong in the family. This lying to them was ripping at her gut.

Yes, she could tell them but when she'd asked about what they knew in regards to her birth parents or if she had blood siblings there had been pain in their eyes. She despised hurting them and so when Jasmine had first contacted her, she'd kept it to herself. And the first meeting. Partly to protect them—if she hadn't gotten along with Jasmine, only Caro would have been hurt.

May not have been the smartest thing to leave without telling them exactly where I was going.

She sat up a bit more as the cab drew to a halt before the Dane County Airport below the Delta sign. Passing the driver as she exited, she handed him a bill. "Keep the change."

"Thank you."

She smiled and walked inside to the first kiosk, bag on her shoulder. Before long she had her boarding ticket and was making her way through to security and on to her gate.

Seated in first class, she used the pillow and blanket provided after storing her bag. She closed her eyes and waited for them to take off, alone in her row. She'd raised the rest between the seats.

The flight was uneventful and she woke with the announcement of flight attendants preparing the cabin for landing. She watched the night lights of Atlanta come into view as they approached the airport.

As they taxied to the terminal gate, she withdrew her bag from beneath the seat ahead of her, her nerves suddenly going wonky. She chewed on the side of her lip and wished that she had her papers — she made origami swans when she got stressed or nervous. As a child she'd read *Sadako and the Thousand Paper Cranes* and had created a thousand of her own and hung them up in her room. It was the only shape she could make but she had the ability to create them from any papers.

The seatbelt light blinked off and she gained her feet, swung her bag in front of her and disembarked. Once firmly in the airport, she sidestepped an employee then sent Terri a text before striking out.

She waited for a taxi and gazed around taking it all in. The night was warm, despite it being autumn.

"The Marriott on Peachtree," she informed the driver as he held the door for her.

"Yes, ma'am."

It didn't take long after arriving for her to secure a room and ride the elevator up to it on the thirty-fourth floor. Bag on the bed, she went to the window and stared out. The golden dome of the capital shone brightly against the night skyline.

* * * *

She spent the next day touring the Underground and sampling Coca-Cola in flavors she'd never imagined. Dinner she ate at one of the restaurants in the hotel then at nine she took a taxi to where Jasmine had told her she'd first visited when she'd moved to the capital city.

Caro got out, paid her fare and strolled into the downtown shopping complex. After making her way to the bookstore she grabbed a small table in the café and sipped the coffee she'd ordered.

A few minutes before the allotted meeting time a woman with a large hat and big sunglasses swept into the seat across from her. The items were removed and Caro frowned. Jasmine.

"Jasmine, what is going on? No more of this cryptic talk."

Jasmine held up a finger then went to order a drink and muffin. Caro stared at her twin. They didn't much look alike currently. Sure there were, of course, similarities but Jasmine's hair was pink—bright pink— now and styled, short and spiky. Her clothing... *I wouldn't be caught dead in that.*

Her skintight jeans looked uncomfortable. The stilettos, while extremely nice, were black as was the tight leather jacket she had on, its numerous zippers catching then reflecting the overhead lights.

Jasmine was hiding something. Granted, she didn't know her all that well, but Caro wasn't about to ignore her suspicions. Her sister returned, hips swaying with every step and sat.

There had been no hug or even a half-hearted attempt at one. Caro drummed her fingers along the rim of her plain coffee and watched Jasmine drink the concoction she had. "Well?" Caro prompted.

"I'm in trouble." Her fingers clenched on the cup. "There are some guys after me."

Unease skittered up her spine. "For what? What do they want and who are the 'guys' that are after you?"

Brown eyes met hers. "Really bad guys, Caro. I didn't want to bring you in but" — she glanced around again — "I hoped you wouldn't mind going with me to talk to the cops." A shrug. "Cop. The one who I've been...dealing with. In fact I'd like you to go for me so I can take care of some things I can't do with five-oh around."

Holding up her hand, Caro shook her head. "What did you do? And what makes you think I would go as you."

"I just told what I saw. It was against a crime boss. His men want to kill me so I can't testify against him."

Crime boss? She had a sinking feeling. "You want me to go in your place to meet some cop?" *I need as much information as I can get here.*

"Officer Declan McBride."

She rolled her eyes and Caro got the feeling these two didn't get along all that well.

"And what, he doesn't believe you?"

Her twin shrugged. "We aren't what you could call the best of friends. He doesn't like me and... Let's just say the feeling is mutual." She drank. "The problem also is he has...certain views about how I am and may not be inclined to believe I will be there to testify."

Caro kept her expression composed. She knew Jasmine's adoptive parents had died and she'd been their only child so when they'd gone, she'd had no one. Jasmine's expression was tortured.

Outrage grew inside her, unfolding like angry tendrils. How dare this man treat her sister this way. It had to be horribly frightening to be expected to testify against a crime boss especially feeling so alone.

"Okay, I'll go in your place. I'll help you, whatever you need. He can think what he wants, we're sisters. Twins. It's what we do for one another. I'll go and you get your stuff done." She finished her coffee. "When and where?"

"Thank you!" Jasmine smiled brightly and touched Caro's hand. "We can do lunch after, it shouldn't take too long. Tomorrow morning. I'm going to need you to hang with him for a short time so I can get a few things taken care of. Things I can't do with a cop hanging around me. But I think if everyone is thinking you're me and I'm, meaning you, are with the cops I can get this stuff done. Then I'll come back and we'll trade off again." She wrote an address down on a napkin and slid it over to her. "We should switch bags as well in case he wants your—my—ID."

Caro hesitated. Give up her bag? *Is this legal?* "Is this why you wanted to meet tonight? Like this? You're scared?"

An indescribable emotion filled her features and Caro had that uncertainty again. Jasmine nodded and ate some of her muffin. "I figured they were listening to me and wouldn't know where I was talking about. I wanted to get your help before I went back to the cops." She fidgeted.

Caro waited a while then finally said, "Why don't you leave if you'd prefer not to be out. Do you have a place to go where you feel safe?" She bit her lip and slid her bag to her twin.

"I do. That's part of what I have to resolve on my own. It's a small hostel but I blend in there. I'm safer there than I would be with the cops. This crime boss has a long reach and I would just assume to not be in his way if he tries to reach out and touch me." She stood. "I have to go. See you tomorrow." She donned her hat and glasses before walking off. Halfway to the door, she wheeled back around. "Thanks for coming."

Caro gave a slight nod and waved. *I should be able to just relax if this only takes until tomorrow. She feels safer away from the cops. Perhaps this one is just incompetent in his job. If that's the case we can always ask for another to be assigned. Something has her spooked.* On her feet she grabbed her cup and the items Jasmine hadn't disposed of. Caro grabbed Jasmine's bag and left to hail another cab.

About the Author

USA Today Bestselling Author Aliyah Burke is an avid reader and is never far from pen and paper (or the computer). She is happily married to a career military man. They are owned by six Borzoi. She spends her days at the day job, writing, and working with her dogs.

Aliyah loves to hear from readers. You can find her contact information, website details and author profile page at https://www.firstforromance.com

ENTWINED PUBLISHING

Made in the USA
Coppell, TX
27 March 2026